CODE TO ZERO

A man wakes up on the floor of a public toilet in Washington, scared and hung over, unable to work out his identity or what has happened to him. All the evidence suggests he is a drunken tramp—yet he knows that can't be true.

Who is he and how did he lose his memory? As he unearths answers, his fear grows. He realises he must, in the depths of his mind, hold information so secret that it has made him a target . . .

CODE TO ZERO

SELECT EDITIONS

This condensation has been created by The Reader's Digest Association Limited by special arrangement with Macmillan Publishers Ltd.

With the exception of actual personages identified as such, the characters and incidents in this volume are entirely the products of the author's imagination and have no relation to any person or events in real life.

The original edition of this book was published and copyrighted as follows: CODE TO ZERO. published at £16.99 by Macmillan © 2000 by Ken Follett. The right of Ken Follett to be identified as the author of this work has been asserted by him in accordance with the Copyright, Designs and Patents Act 1988. Cover images and front cover/spine of slipcase photomontage (far right): Hulton Getty; The Photographers Library; photomontage by John Calvert. Author photo on page 143: Barbara Follett. Slipcase photomontage by Shark Attack.

The Reader's Digest Association Limited,
11 Westferry Circus, Canary Wharf, London E14 4HE.

www.readersdigest.co.uk
ISBN 0 276 42541 3

Printed and bound by GGP Media, Pössneck, Germany

KEN FOLLETT
CODE TO ZERO

READER'S DIGEST SELECT EDITIONS
CONDENSED BOOKS DIVISION

Historical note: *The launch of the first American space satellite, Explorer I, was originally scheduled for Wednesday, January 29, 1958. Late that evening, it was postponed to the following day. The reason given was the weather. Observers at Cape Canaveral were puzzled: it was a perfect, sunny Florida day. Next night, there was another postponement, and the same reason was given.*

The launch was finally attempted on Friday, January 31.

Part One

5.00am: He woke up scared.

Worse than that: he was terrified. His heart was pounding, his breath came in gasps and his body was taut. It was like a nightmare, except that waking brought no sense of relief. He felt that something dreadful had happened, but he did not know what it was.

He opened his eyes. A faint light illuminated his surroundings, and he made out vague shapes. Somewhere near by, water ran. He tried to make himself calm and attempted to think straight. He was lying on a hard floor. He was cold, and he had some kind of hangover, with a headache and a dry mouth and a feeling of nausea.

He sat upright, shaking with fear. There was an unpleasant smell of disinfectant. He recognised the outline of a row of washbasins. He was in a public toilet.

He felt disgusted. He had been sleeping on the floor of a men's room. What the hell had happened to him? He concentrated. He was fully dressed, wearing some kind of topcoat and heavy boots, though he had a feeling that these were not his clothes. His panic was subsiding, but in its place came a deeper fear.

He needed light. He got to his feet and peered into the gloom. Holding his arms out in front of him in case of invisible obstacles, he made his way to a wall. Then he walked crabwise, his hands exploring. He found a cold glassy surface he guessed was a mirror, then a towel roller. At last his fingertips touched a switch, and he turned it on.

Bright light flooded white-tiled walls. In a corner was what looked like a bundle of old clothes. He asked himself how he got here. What had happened last night? He could not remember. *He could not remember anything at all.*

What was his name? He did not know.

He turned towards the mirror. He saw a filthy hobo, dressed in rags, with matted hair, a dirty face and a crazy stare. Then he was hit by a terrible revelation. The hobo was himself. In a voice that shook with terror, he shouted, 'Who am I?'

The bundle of old clothes moved and a voice mumbled, 'You're a bum, Luke. Pipe down.'

His name was Luke. He was grateful for the knowledge. A name was not much, but it gave him a focus. He stared at his companion. The man wore a ripped tweed coat with string for a belt. He rubbed his eyes and muttered, 'My head hurts.'

Luke said, 'Who are you?'

'I'm Pete, you retard, can't you see?'

Luke swallowed. 'I've lost my memory!'

'I ain't surprised. You drank most of a bottle of bourbon yesterday. It's a miracle you didn't lose your entire mind.'

Bourbon would explain the hangover, Luke thought. 'But why would I drink a whole bottle?'

Pete laughed. 'That's about the dumbest question I ever heard. To get drunk, of course!'

Luke was appalled. He was a drunken bum who slept in public toilets. He bent over a washbasin, ran the cold water, and drank from the tap. It made him feel better. He wiped his mouth, then forced himself to look in the mirror again. The reflection showed a man in his late thirties, with dark hair and blue eyes. He had no beard or moustache, just a heavy growth of dark stubble.

He turned back to his companion. 'Luke what?' he said. 'What's my last name?'

'How the hell am I supposed to know?' Pete got to his feet. 'I need some breakfast.'

Luke realised he was hungry. He searched his pockets for money. All were empty. 'I think I'm broke,' he said.

'No kidding,' Pete said sarcastically. 'Come on.' He stumbled through a doorway. Luke followed.

When he emerged into the light, he suffered another shock. He was in a huge temple, empty and eerily silent. Mahogany benches stood in rows on the marble floor, like church pews waiting for a ghostly congregation. The insane thought crossed Luke's mind that he had been the sacrificial victim in a weird rite that had left him with no memory. 'What is this place?' he asked.

'Union Station, Washington, DC,' said Pete.

Luke felt foolish. He was in a grandiose train station, early in the morning before it filled up with passengers. He had scared himself, like a child imagining monsters in a dark bedroom.

Pete headed for an arch marked EXIT, and Luke hurried after him.

An aggressive voice called, 'Hey! Hey, you!'

Pete said, 'Oh-oh.' He quickened his step.

A stout man in a railroad uniform bore down on them, full of righteous indignation. 'You bums been sleeping here, ain't you?' he said. 'You know that ain't allowed.'

Luke suppressed a retort and walked faster.

'This ain't a flophouse,' the man went on. 'Now scat.' He shoved Luke's shoulder.

Luke turned suddenly. 'Don't touch me!' he said.

The man took a big step backward, looking scared.

Pete took Luke's arm. 'Let's go.'

They passed through the arch. It was dark outside. The air was bitterly cold, and Luke drew his ragged clothes closer about him. It was winter, maybe January or February. He wondered what year it was. Pete turned left, apparently sure where he was going. Luke followed.

'Where are we headed?' he asked.

'I know a gospel shop on H Street where we can get free breakfast, so long as you don't mind singing a hymn or two.'

'I'm starving—I'll sing a whole oratorio.'

Luke's mind seethed with anxious questions. How long had he been a drunk? Did he have any family? Where had he met Pete? But Pete was taciturn, and Luke controlled his impatience, hoping Pete might be more forthcoming when he had some food inside him.

They came to a small church between a cinema and a liquor store. They entered by a side door and went down to the basement. At one end of a long low room Luke saw a piano and a small pulpit; at the other, a kitchen range. In between were trestle tables with benches. At the kitchen end, a woman stirred a big pot. Beside her, a grey-bearded man wearing a clerical collar looked up from a coffee urn and smiled. 'Come in, come in,' he said cheerfully.

'Morning, Pastor Lonegan,' Pete said.

'You're a little early for breakfast, but there's fresh coffee.' The pastor poured it into thick mugs. 'Milk and sugar?'

Luke did not know whether he liked milk and sugar in his coffee. 'Yes, thank you,' he said, guessing. He sipped the coffee. It tasted sickeningly creamy and sweet. He guessed he normally took it black. But it assuaged his hunger, and he drank it all quickly.

Luke and Pete sat at a table and Luke studied his companion. Until now, he had noticed only the dirty face and ragged clothes. Now he saw that Pete had none of the marks of a long-term drunk: no broken veins, no flaking skin, no cuts or bruises. Perhaps he was too young—only about twenty-five, Luke guessed. He had a dark red birthmark that ran from his right ear to his jaw line.

'What are you staring at?' Pete said.

Luke shrugged and did not reply. On the table was a newspaper folded open at the crossword, and a pencil. Luke picked up the pencil, and started to fill in the answers.

More bums drifted in. Luke got all the crossword clues but one,

'Small place in Denmark,' six letters. Pastor Lonegan looked over his shoulder and said quietly to his wife, 'Oh, what a noble mind is here o'erthrown!' Luke immediately got the clue. HAMLET, he wrote in. Then he thought, How did I know that?

He unfolded the paper and looked at the front page. It was dated Wednesday, January 29, 1958. His eye was caught by the headline: US MOON STAYS EARTHBOUND.

> Cape Canaveral, Tuesday: The US Navy abandoned a second attempt to launch its space rocket, Vanguard, after technical problems. American hopes of launching a satellite to rival the Soviet Sputnik now rest with the Army's Jupiter missile.

The piano sounded a strident chord. Mrs Lonegan was playing a familiar hymn, 'What a Friend we have in Jesus'. Luke joined in the singing, pleased he could remember the song. Bourbon had a strange effect, he thought. He could do the crossword and sing a hymn from memory, but he did not know his mother's name.

After the hymn, they said grace. Then the men lined up and Mrs Lonegan served them hot oatmeal. Luke ate three bowls. Afterwards, feeling better, he approached the pastor. 'Sir, have you seen me here before? I've lost my memory.'

Lonegan looked at him. 'I don't believe I have. How old are you?'

'I don't know,' Luke said, feeling foolish.

'Late thirties, I'd say. You haven't been living rough very long. It takes its toll on a man. But you're alert enough to do a crossword puzzle. Quit drinking now, and you could lead a normal life again.'

Luke wondered how many times the pastor had said that. 'I'm going to try,' he promised.

'If you need help, just ask.' A young man who appeared to be mentally handicapped was patting Lonegan's arm, and he turned to him with a patient smile.

Luke spoke to Pete. 'How long have you known me?'

'I don't know. You been around a while. Relax, will you? Your memory will come back sooner or later.'

'I have to find out where I'm from.'

Pete hesitated. 'What we need is a beer. Help us think straight.' He turned for the door.

Luke grabbed his arm. 'I don't want a beer,' he said decisively. Pete did not want him to dig into his past, it seemed. 'In fact, I think I'd like to be alone for a while.'

'What are you, Greta Garbo?'

'I'm serious.'

'You need me to look out for you. You can't make it on your own. Hell, you can't even remember how old you are.'

Pete had a desperate look in his eyes, but Luke was unmoved. 'I appreciate your concern, but you're not helping me find out who I am.'

Pete shrugged. 'You got a right. See you around, maybe.'

'Maybe.'

Pete went out. Luke thanked Pastor Lonegan, then went up the stairs and out into the street. Pete was on the next block, speaking to a man in a green gaberdine raincoat—begging the price of a beer, Luke guessed. He turned and walked in the opposite direction.

It was still dark. Luke's feet were cold. He realised he wasn't wearing socks. As he hurried on, a light flurry of snow fell. After a few minutes, he eased his pace. He had no reason to rush.

6.00AM: ELSPETH WOKE up worrying about Luke. She lay in bed for a few moments, her heart heavy with concern for the man she loved. Then she switched on the bedside lamp and sat upright.

Her motel room was decorated with a space-programme theme. The floor lamp was shaped like a rocket, and the pictures on the wall showed planets, crescent moons and orbital paths in a wildly unrealistic night sky. The Starlite was one of a cluster of new motels that had sprouted in the area of Cocoa Beach, Florida, eight miles south of Cape Canaveral. The decorator had obviously thought the space theme appropriate, but it made Elspeth feel as if she were borrowing the bedroom of a ten-year-old boy.

She picked up the bedside phone and dialled Anthony Carroll's office in Washington, DC. At the other end, the phone rang unanswered. She tried his home number with the same result. Had something gone wrong? She felt sick with fear. She would call his office again in half an hour.

As she showered, she thought about Luke and Anthony when she had first known them. They were at Harvard and she was at

Radcliffe, before the war. Best friends, Luke and Anthony had made an odd couple. Both were tall and athletic, but there the resemblance ended. The Radcliffe girls had called them Beauty and the Beast. Luke was Beauty, with his wavy black hair and elegant clothes. Anthony was not handsome, but girls were attracted to his energy and intense enthusiasm.

Elspeth showered quickly. In her bathrobe, she sat at the dressing table to do her make-up. She had been sitting at a dressing table wearing a bathrobe the first time she ever spoke to Luke. It was during a panty raid by a group of Harvard boys. By chance, Luke had come to her room. He was a maths major, like her. Once alone with her, Luke had seemed embarrassed. She had smiled, pointed to the closet, and said, 'Top drawer.' He had taken a pair of pretty white panties with a lace edging. The next day he asked her for a date.

She tried to concentrate on her make-up. The job was more difficult than usual this morning, because she had slept badly. She had a maths degree from Radcliffe, but still she was expected to look like a mannequin at work. She brushed her hair. It was reddish-brown, and cut in the fashionable style: chin-length and turned under at the back. She dressed quickly in a green-and-tan striped shirtwaist.

She picked up the phone and dialled Anthony's office again. There was no reply.

1941: ELSPETH TWOMEY had fallen in love with Luke the first time he kissed her.

That had been six months ago, and the feeling had grown stronger since. Now she was seeing Luke almost every day. They were both in their senior year. Every day they either met for lunch or studied together. Weekends they spent almost all their time together.

It was not uncommon for Radcliffe girls to get engaged in their final year, to a Harvard boy or a young professor. But Luke had never spoken about marriage.

She looked at him now, sitting in a booth at the back of Flanagan's Bar, arguing with Bern Rothsten, a graduate student. Bern was a communist, like many Harvard students and professors.

'Your father's a banker,' he said to Luke with disdain. 'You'll be a banker, too. Of course you think capitalism is great.'

Elspeth saw a flush rise at Luke's throat. His father had recently been featured in a *Time* magazine article as one of ten men who had become millionaires since the Depression.

Luke said, 'Banking is an honourable job. Bankers help people.'

'Like they did in 1929.'

'They make mistakes. Soldiers make mistakes—they shoot the wrong people—but I don't accuse you of being a murderer.'

It was Bern's turn to look wounded. He had fought in the Spanish Civil War—he was older than the rest of them—and Elspeth now guessed he was remembering some tragic error.

Luke added, 'Anyway, I don't aim to be a banker.'

Bern's dowdy girlfriend, Peg, leaned forward, interested. Like Bern she was intense in her convictions, but she did not have his sarcastic tongue. 'What, then?'

'A scientist. I want to explore beyond our planet.'

Bern laughed scornfully. 'Space rockets! A schoolboy fantasy.'

Elspeth leaped to Luke's defence. 'Knock it off, Bern. You don't know what you're talking about.'

'I think it's going to happen,' Luke said. 'And I believe science will do more than communism for ordinary people in our lifetime.'

Elspeth winced. She felt Luke was naive about politics. 'The benefits of science are restricted to the privileged elite,' she said.

'That's not true,' Luke said.

A tall figure cast a shadow over the table. 'Are you kids old enough to drink alcoholic liquor?' It was Anthony Carroll. With him was someone so striking that Elspeth uttered an involuntary murmur of surprise. She was a small girl, fashionably dressed in a short red jacket, with curls of dark hair escaping from under a little red hat. 'Meet Billie Josephson,' said Anthony.

Luke stood up to shake hands and knocked over a glass. It was unusual for him to be clumsy, and Elspeth realised with annoyance that he was taken with Miss Josephson. 'I'm surprised,' he said, giving her his most charming smile. 'When Anthony said his date was called Billie, I imagined someone six feet tall and built like a wrestler.'

Billie laughed and slid into the booth beside Luke. 'My name is

Bilhah,' she said. 'It's biblical, she was the handmaiden of Jacob and the mother of Dan. But I was brought up in Dallas, where they called me Billie-Jo.'

Anthony sat next to Elspeth and said quietly, 'Isn't she pretty?'

Billie was not exactly pretty, Elspeth thought. She had a sharp nose and large, intense, dark-brown eyes. It was the whole package that was so stunning: the angle of the hat, the Texas accent, and most of all her animation. While she talked to Luke, telling him some tall story, she smiled, frowned, and pantomimed all kinds of emotion.

'She's cute,' Elspeth said to Anthony. 'How did you meet her?'

'I noticed her in the Fogg Museum. She was wearing a green coat with brass buttons and a beret. I thought she looked like a toy soldier fresh out of the box.'

Billie was not a toy, Elspeth thought. She was more dangerous than that. Billie laughed at something Luke had said and swiped his arm in mock admonishment. Irritated, Elspeth interrupted them and said to Billie, 'Are you planning to beat the curfew tonight?'

Radcliffe girls were supposed to be in their dormitories by ten o'clock. To stay out later they had to put their name in a book with details of where they planned to go and what time they would be back. Billie said, 'I'm supposed to be spending the night with a visiting aunt who has taken a suite at the Ritz. What's your story?'

'No story, just a ground-floor window that will be left open.'

Billie said, 'In fact, I'm staying with friends of Anthony's.'

'Some people my mother knows, who have a large apartment,' Anthony said to Elspeth. 'Don't give me that old-fashioned look, they're terribly respectable.'

'I should hope so,' Elspeth said primly, and she had the satisfaction of seeing Billie blush. Turning to Luke, she said, 'Honey, what time's the movie?'

He looked at his wristwatch. 'We've got to go,' he said.

Luke had borrowed a Ford roadster for the weekend. They drove into Boston to see Alfred Hitchcock's latest film, *Suspicion*.

Around midnight they returned to Cambridge and pulled off Memorial Drive to park facing the Charles River, next to the boathouse. The car had no heater, and Elspeth turned up the fur collar of her coat and leaned against Luke for warmth.

They talked about the movie. Elspeth thought that in real life the Joan Fontaine character, a repressed girl brought up by stuffy parents, would never be attracted to the kind of ne'er-do-well Cary Grant had played. Luke said, 'But that's why she fell for him—because he was dangerous.'

Elspeth looked at the reflection of the moon on the water. Billie Josephson was dangerous, she thought.

Luke changed the subject. 'This afternoon, Professor Davies told me I could do my master's degree right here at Harvard.'

'What made him say that?'

'I mentioned that I was hoping to go to Columbia. He said, "What for? Stay here!" I explained that my family's in New York.'

Luke was the eldest of four children. His mother was French. Elspeth knew that Luke was fond of his two teenage brothers and doted on his eleven-year-old sister.

'Professor Davies is a bachelor,' she said. 'He lives for his work.'

'Have you thought about doing a master's?' he asked. 'You're a better mathematician than most of the Harvard men.'

'I've always wanted to work at the State Department.'

'That would mean living in Washington.'

Elspeth was sure Luke was just thinking aloud, but he seemed dismayed that they might move to different cities.

'Have you ever been in love?' he said suddenly.

'When I was seventeen, there was a steelworks dispute in Chicago,' she said. 'I was very political in those days. I went to help as a volunteer. I worked for a young organiser called Jack Largo, and I fell in love with him.'

'And he with you?'

'Goodness, no. He was twenty-five; he thought of me as a kid.' She hesitated. 'He kissed me once, though. We were packing leaflets, and I said something that made him laugh. "You're a gem, Ellie," he said. Then he kissed me. I nearly died of joy. But he just went on packing leaflets as though nothing had changed.'

'Are you still in touch with him?'

She shook her head. 'He was killed.' She fought back sudden

tears. 'Two off-duty policemen, hired by the steelworks, got him in an alley and beat him to death with iron bars.'

'No!' Luke stared at her.

'Everyone in town knew who had done it, but nobody was arrested.'

He took her hand. 'I've read about that kind of stuff in the papers but it never seemed real.'

'It's real. The mills must keep rolling. Anyone who gets in the way has to be rubbed out.'

'You make it sound as if industry were no better than organised crime.'

'I don't see a big difference. But I don't get involved any more. That was enough.' Luke had started talking about love, but she had stupidly moved the conversation on to politics. She switched back. 'What about you?' she said. 'Have you ever been in love?'

'I don't think I know what love is.' It was a typical boy's answer. But then he kissed her and she relaxed. After a while he drew away from her and sighed. 'I wonder how married people ever get bored. They never have to stop.'

'Their children stop them, I guess,' she said with a laugh.

'Do you want to have children, some day?'

She felt her breath come faster. 'Of course I do.'

He turned to her with a serious expression. 'I'd like four. How would you feel about that? Having four children?'

She smiled happily. 'If they were yours, I'd love it,' she said.

He kissed her again.

Soon it became too cold to stay where they were, and reluctantly they drove back towards the Radcliffe dorms. As they were passing through Harvard Square, a figure waved to them from the side of the road. 'Is that Anthony?' Luke said incredulously.

It was, Elspeth saw. Billie was with him.

Luke pulled over, and Anthony came to the window. 'I'm glad I spotted you,' he said. 'I need a favour. My friends have gone away—they must have got the dates mixed up. Billie has nowhere to go.'

Billie had lied about where she was spending the night, Elspeth recalled. Now she could not return to her dorm without revealing her deception.

'I took her to the House.' He meant Cambridge House, where he and Luke lived. 'I thought she could sleep in our room, and Luke and I could spend the night in the library.'

Elspeth said, 'You're crazy.'

Luke put in, 'It's been done before. So what went wrong?'

'We were seen.'

'Oh, no,' Elspeth said. For a girl to be found in a man's room was a serious offence. Both of them could be expelled.

Luke said, 'Who saw you?'

'Geoff Pidgeon and a whole bunch of men. It was half dark and they were all drunk. I'll talk to them in the morning.'

Luke nodded. 'What are you going to do now?'

'Billie has a cousin who lives in Newport, Rhode Island. Would you drive her there?'

'What?' said Elspeth. 'But it's fifty miles away!'

'What do you say, Luke?' Anthony asked.

'Of course,' Luke said.

Elspeth had known he would comply. It was a matter of honour for him to help a friend. But she was angry all the same.

'Hey, thanks,' Anthony said lightly.

'No problem,' Luke said. 'Well, there is a problem. This car is a two-seater.'

Elspeth opened the door and got out. 'Be my guest,' she said sulkily. She hated the thought of Luke spending two hours in this little car with sexy Billie Josephson.

Luke sensed her displeasure and said, 'Elspeth, get back in, I'll drive you home first.'

'No need,' she said. 'Anthony can walk me to the dorm.'

'I don't know how to thank you,' Billie said to Elspeth. She got into the car and closed the door.

Luke waved and drove off.

Anthony and Elspeth stood and watched the car recede into the darkness.

6.30AM: DAYLIGHT CREPT stealthily over the cold city. Men and women came out of houses, narrowing their eyes against the biting wind, and hurried towards the warmth and bright lights of offices.

Luke had no destination: one street was as good as another when none of them meant anything. He began to study the people he passed. He kept hoping that one of them would stop, and say, 'Luke, what happened to you? Come home with me, let me help you!' He began to feel he was not going to be lucky. Walking around fantasising about a lucky break was no kind of strategy. He needed a plan.

He wondered if he might be a Missing Person. There was a list, he felt sure, of such people. Who kept the list? It had to be the police. Or, if not, they would know.

He seemed to remember passing a precinct house a few minutes earlier. He turned abruptly to go back. As he did so, he bumped into a young man in an olive-coloured gaberdine raincoat. He had a feeling he might have seen the man before. Their eyes met, but the man looked away, and walked on. Swallowing his disappointment, Luke tried to retrace his steps. It was difficult, because he had turned corners and crossed streets more or less at random. However, he had to come across a police station sooner or later.

Soon he had completely lost his way. He was on a street of cheap shops. He stopped suddenly and looked back. Thirty yards behind him, he saw the man in a green gaberdine raincoat, watching the TV in a store window. Luke frowned, thinking, 'Is he shadowing me?'

It was easy enough to check. Luke walked to the end of the block, crossed the street, and walked back along the other side. When he reached the far end he stood at the kerb and looked both ways. The olive raincoat was thirty yards behind him. Luke crossed again. To allay suspicion, he studied doors as if looking for a street number. The raincoat followed.

Luke was mystified, but his heart leaped with hope. A man who was following him must know something about him—maybe even his identity.

For a real test to see if he was being followed, he needed to travel in a vehicle, forcing his shadow to do the same. Now he needed the bus fare. He began to look at his surroundings with different eyes. He saw newsstands to be robbed, handbags that could be snatched, pockets ready to be picked. He stepped inside a coffee shop.

His eyes raked the tables, looking for change left as tips. He approached the counter. A radio was playing the news. 'Rocket experts claim America has one last chance of catching up with the Russians in the race to control outer space.'

The counterman was making espresso coffee, and a delicious fragrance make Luke's nostrils flare.

What would a bum say? 'Any stale doughnuts?' he asked.

'Get out of here,' the man said roughly.

Luke saw what he needed. Beside the till, within easy reach, was a can with a slit in the top and the label saying: REMEMBER THOSE WHO CANNOT SEE. Now Luke just had to distract the counterman.

'Gimme a dime?' he said.

The man said, 'OK, that's it, you get the bum's rush.' But he had to duck under the counter to get out, and for a second he could not see Luke. In that moment, Luke took the collection box and slipped it inside his coat.

The counterman grabbed Luke by the collar and propelled him rapidly across the café. At the door the man gave him a painful kick.

In an alleyway, Luke busted the can open. The money inside, mostly pennies, amounted to two or three dollars, he guessed. He put it in his coat pocket and returned to the street. He thanked heaven for charity and made a silent promise to give three bucks to the blind if he ever got straight. All right, he thought, thirty bucks.

The man in the olive raincoat was standing by a newsstand.

A bus pulled up a few yards away. Luke had no idea where it went, but he boarded. The driver gave him a hard look. 'The fare is seventeen cents, unless you got a token,' he said. Luke paid with some of the change he had stolen. As he walked towards the back of the bus, he looked anxiously out of the window. The man in the raincoat was walking away. Luke frowned. The man should have been trying to hail a taxicab. Maybe he was not a shadow, after all.

The bus pulled away, and Luke took a seat.

At the third stop, Luke got off the bus. He looked up and down the street. There was no sign of the man in the olive raincoat. As he hesitated, he noticed that one of the passengers who had got off the bus with him had paused in a shop doorway and was fumbling in his pockets. As Luke watched, he lit a cigarette and took a long, satisfying drag. He was a tall man, wearing a grey Homburg hat.

Luke realised he had seen him before.

7.00AM: ANTHONY CARROLL drove along Constitution Avenue in a five-year-old Cadillac Eldorado. He pulled into the parking lot of Q Building in Alphabet Row, a strip of barracks-like structures hastily erected, during the war, on parkland near the Lincoln Memorial. He had spent much of the war here, working for the Office of Strategic Services, precursor of the CIA. A multimillion-dollar CIA headquarters was under construction across the Potomac River in Langley, Virginia. When it was completed, Alphabet Row would be demolished.

Anthony was a hugely powerful figure within the Agency. He was Head of Technical Services, a euphemistic name for the division responsible for burglary, phone tapping, and other illegal activities. Its nickname was Dirty Tricks. Anthony's position was founded on his record as a war hero, and a series of Cold War coups. However, he had enemies: pen-pushers who disliked the whole notion of the government doing secret operations. They were ready to destroy him as soon as he made a slip. And today his neck was stuck out further than ever before.

As he strode into the building, he focused on the problem of the day: Dr Claude Lucas, known as Luke, the most dangerous man in America, the one who threatened everything Anthony had lived for.

He had been at the office most of the night, and had gone home only to shave and change his shirt. The guard in the lobby said, 'Mr Maxell's in your office, sir.'

Anthony frowned. Pete Maxell was supposed to be with Luke. Had something gone wrong? He ran up the stairs.

Pete was sitting in the chair opposite Anthony's desk, still dressed in ragged clothes, a smear of dirt partly covering his birthmark. As Anthony walked in he jumped up, looking scared.

'What happened?' Anthony said.

'Luke decided he wanted to be alone. But Simons has him under surveillance, and Betts is there for back-up.'

'What about his memory.'

'Completely gone.'

Anthony took off his coat and sat behind his desk. He looked at the man opposite. Pete was a good agent, but inexperienced. However, he was fanatically loyal to Anthony.

Anthony said, 'Tell me exactly what happened.'

Pete sat down again. 'He woke up crazy, yelling "Who am I?" and stuff like that. I made a mistake: I called him Luke.'

Anthony had told Pete to observe Luke but not to give him any information. 'No matter—it's not his real name.'

'Then he asked who I was, and I said, "I'm Pete." It just came out, I was so concerned to stop him yelling. He asked questions. "How long have I been like this?" "Do I have any family?" I kept trying to steer him away from enquiring into his past. But I think he figured out what I was doing.'

'Where is he *now*?' Anthony asked.

'I don't know. Steve will call in as soon as he gets a chance.'

'When he does, get back there and join up with him. Whatever happens, Luke mustn't get away from us.'

The white phone on Anthony's desk rang, his direct line. He stared at it. Not many people had the number. He picked it up.

'It's me,' said Elspeth's voice. 'What's happened?'

'Relax,' he said. 'Everything is under control.'

7.30AM: THE SHADOW followed Luke for a quarter of a mile. It was now full light and, although the street was busy, Luke easily kept track of the grey Homburg hat, but after he crossed Pennsylvania Avenue it disappeared from view. Once again, he wondered if he might be imagining things. But a minute later he spotted the green raincoat coming out of a bakery.

'You again,' he said under his breath. There was no further room for doubt: two people were following him in a smoothly executed relay operation. They had to be professionals. He tried to figure out what that meant. They could be spies, KGB or CIA, although it seemed unlikely that a deadbeat could be involved in espionage.

He decided he would split the team then confront one of the men. He stepped into a shop and bought a pack of Pall Malls.

When he went outside, Raincoat had disappeared and Homburg had taken over again. He walked to the end of the block and turned the corner.

A Coca-Cola truck was parked at the kerb, and the driver was unloading crates. Luke walked to the far side of the truck, dropped to the ground and rolled under it. Looking along the sidewalk at ground level, he picked out the blue suit pants and tan oxfords of his shadow.

The man quickened his pace, presumably concerned that Luke had disappeared. He walked around the truck, then returned to the sidewalk and broke into a run.

Luke was pleased. He did not know how he had learned this game, but he seemed to be good at it. He crawled to the front of the truck and scrambled to his feet. Homburg was still hurrying away.

Luke crossed the sidewalk and turned the corner. He stood in the doorway of an electrical store, opened the pack of cigarettes, and took one out.

Raincoat appeared. He spotted Luke, gave a nervous start, and continued walking, edging to the outside of the sidewalk.

Luke stepped into his path and said, 'Got a light, buddy?'

Raincoat hesitated, then stopped. 'Sure,' he said, trying to act casual. He reached into the pocket of his raincoat, took out a book of matches and struck one.

Luke said, 'You know who I am, don't you?'

The man stared at Luke, dumbstruck, until the match burned down. Then he dropped it and said, 'I don't know what you're talking about, pal.'

'You're following me,' Luke said. 'You must know who I am.'

'I'm not following anyone.'

The man tried to walk past Luke. Luke moved sideways, blocking his path. 'Excuse me, please,' Raincoat said.

Frustrated, Luke grabbed him by the lapels of the raincoat and slammed him against the shop window, rattling the glass.

'Get your damn hands off me,' the man said. 'I'm not following you.'

'Who am I?' Luke screamed at him. 'Tell me, who am I?'

'How should I know?'

Luke took the man by the throat. 'You're going to tell me.'

Behind Luke, the frightened voice of a passer-by said, 'Hey, what's going on here?'

Luke let his hands fall to his side. Raincoat backed away. 'You crazy bastard,' he said. 'You're out of your mind.'

'You're lying,' Luke yelled. He reached out to grab the man again.

Raincoat turned and ran away. Luke could have chased him, but he hesitated. What was the point?

After a moment, Luke walked away, heading in the direction opposite to that taken by his two shadows. 'Great job,' he said to himself. 'You achieved precisely nothing.'

And he was alone again.

8.00AM: DR BILLIE JOSEPHSON was running late. She had got her mother up and sat her in the kitchen with coffee. She woke her seven-year-old, Larry, then returned to the kitchen.

Her mother, a small, plump woman of seventy known as Becky-Ma, had the radio on loud. Perry Como was singing 'Catch a Falling Star'. Billie put bread in the toaster for her mother and poured cornflakes into a bowl for Larry. Then she made a peanut butter and jelly sandwich for Larry's lunch. She put the lunch box in his school bag and added his baseball glove, a present from his father.

On the radio, a reporter was interviewing sightseers on the beach near Cape Canaveral who were hoping to see a rocket launch.

Larry came into the kitchen. She got him started on his cornflakes, and began to scramble eggs.

The radio reporter was interviewing an army spokesman. 'What if the rocket goes off course and crash-lands right here on the beach?'

'There's no danger of that,' came the reply. 'Every rocket has a self-destruct mechanism. If it veers off course it will be blown up in midair.'

'But how can you blow it up after it's already taken off?'

'The explosive device is triggered by a radio signal sent by the range safety officer.'

Larry said, 'Can I take the yoghurt pot to school?'

'No, you can't. It's half full,' she told him.

'But I have to take some containers! Miss Page will be mad if I don't.' He was near to tears with the suddenness of a seven-year-old.

'What do you need containers for?'

'To make a space rocket! She told us last week.'

Billie sighed. 'Larry, if you had told *me* last week, I would have saved a whole bunch for you. What kind of containers do you want?'

'Rocket shape.'

Billie went around the house and got a cardboard detergent container, a liquid soap bottle, and an ice-cream tub. Most of the packages showed families using the products—a pretty housewife, two kids, and a pipe-smoking father in the background. She had never lived in a family like that. Her father, a poor tailor in Dallas, had died when she was a baby, and her mother had brought up five children in poverty. Billie herself had been divorced since Larry was two.

She put all the containers in a bag for Larry to carry to school.

'Oh, boy, I bet I have more than anyone,' he said. 'Thanks, Mom.'

A car horn tooted outside, and Billie quickly checked her appearance in the glass of a cupboard door. Her curly black hair had been hastily combed, she had no make-up on and she was wearing an oversize pink sweater . . . but the effect was kind of sexy.

The back door opened and Roy Brodsky came in. Roy was Larry's best friend. He was followed by his father, Harold, a good-looking man with soft brown eyes. Harold Brodsky was a widower, who taught chemistry at the George Washington University. Billie and Harold were dating. He looked at her adoringly and said, 'My God, you look gorgeous.' She grinned and kissed his cheek.

Like Larry, Roy had a bag full of cartons. Billie said to Harold, 'Did you have to empty half the containers in your kitchen?'

'Yes. I have little bowls of soap flakes, and six toilet rolls without the cardboard cylinder.'

'Darn, I never thought of toilet rolls!'

He laughed. 'I wonder, would you like to have dinner at my place tonight?'

She was surprised. 'You're going to cook?'

'Not exactly. I thought I'd ask Mrs Riley to make a casserole. Roy's going to a cousin's birthday party tonight, and he'll sleep over. We'll have a chance to talk without interruption.'

'That'll be great,' Billie said.

'I'll pick you up around eight. Come on, boys.' He shepherded the children out through the back door.

Billie cleared the table. Rushing now, she stripped the beds and bundled the sheets into a laundry bag. She showed Becky-Ma the bag and said, 'Hand this to the laundry man when he calls, OK, Ma?'

Her mother said, 'I don't have any of my heart pills left.'

'Jesus Christ!' She rarely swore in front of her mother, but she was at the end of her rope. 'Ma, I have a busy day at work today and I don't have time to go to the pharmacist!'

'I can't help it, I ran out.' She started to cry.

Billie relented immediately. 'I'm sorry, Ma,' she said. Five years ago, when the three of them had set up house together, Ma had helped take care of Larry. But nowadays she was barely able to look after him when he came home from school.

The phone rang. She picked it up. It was Bern Rothsten, her ex-husband. Billie got on well with him, despite the divorce. 'Hey, Bern—you're up early.'

'Yeah. Have you heard from Luke?'

'Luke Lucas? Lately? No—is something wrong?'

'I don't know, maybe.'

Bern and Luke shared the intimacy of rivals. When they were young they had argued endlessly yet they had remained close at college and all through the war. 'What's happened?' Billie said.

'He called me on Monday. I was kind of surprised. I don't hear from him often.'

'Nor do I.' Billie struggled to remember. 'Last time I saw him was a couple of years ago, I think. Why did he call you?'

'He was coming to Washington and wanted to see me. Something had happened.'

'Did he tell you what?'

'Not really. He just said, "It's like the stuff we did in the war."'

Billie frowned anxiously. Luke and Bern had been in OSS during the war, working behind enemy lines, helping the French Resistance. 'What do you think he meant?'

'I don't know. He said he would call me when he reached Washington. He checked into the Carlton on Monday night. Now it's Wednesday, and he hasn't called. Call me if you hear from him, OK?'

'Sure, of course.'

'Be seeing you.'

'Bye.' Billie hung up. Then she sat at the kitchen table, her chores forgotten, thinking about Luke.

1941: ROUTE 138 MEANDERED south through Massachusetts towards Rhode Island. The old Ford had no heater. Billie was wrapped up in coat, scarf and gloves, but her feet were numb. However, it was no great hardship to spend a couple of hours in a car alone with Luke Lucas, even if he was someone else's boyfriend.

They talked about the war in Europe. That morning in Radcliffe Yard, rival student groups had handed out leaflets, the Interventionists passionately advocating that America should enter the war, the America Firsters opposing it.

'I have cousins in Paris,' Luke said. 'I'd like us to go over there and rescue them. But that's a personal reason.'

'I have a personal reason too: I'm Jewish,' Billie said. 'But rather than send Americans to die in Europe, I'd open our doors to refugees. Save lives instead of killing people.'

'That's what Anthony believes.'

Billie was still fuming about the night's fiasco. 'Anthony should have made sure we could stay at his friends' apartment,' she said.

She was hoping for sympathy from Luke, but he disappointed her. 'I guess you both were a little too casual about the whole thing.'

Billie was stung. 'I think Anthony had a duty to protect my reputation.'

'Yes, but so did you.'

She was surprised he was so critical. 'I'll never do that again, with any man,' she said vehemently.

'Could I ask you a personal question?' Luke met her eyes for a moment. 'Are you in love with Anthony?'

'I'm fond of him, I enjoy his company, but I don't love him.' She thought about Luke's girlfriend, the most striking beauty on campus. 'What about you? Are you in love with Elspeth?'

'To be honest, this is as close to love as I've ever come, but I don't know if it's the real thing.'

'Didn't you put Elspeth in a vulnerable situation tonight, too, keeping her out in your car until the early hours?'

To her surprise, he laughed appreciatively. 'You're right, and I'm a pompous idiot,' he said. 'We all took risks.'

'That's the truth.' She shuddered. 'I don't know what I'd do if I got thrown out.'

'Study somewhere else, I guess.'

She shook her head. 'I'm on a scholarship. My father's dead, my mother's a penniless widow. I couldn't study anywhere without a scholarship. Why do you look surprised?'

'I have to say you don't dress like a scholarship girl.'

'It's the Leavenworth Award,' she explained.

'Wow.' The Leavenworth was a famously generous grant and thousands of outstanding students applied for it. 'You must be a genius.'

'I don't know about that,' she said. 'I'm not smart enough to make sure I have a place to stay the night.'

'On the other hand, being thrown out of college is not the worst thing in the world.'

'It would be the end of the world for me. I want to help sick people get well.'

'You're going to be a doctor?'

'Psychologist. I want to understand how the mind works. It's so mysterious and complicated. Things like logic, the way we think. Imagining something that isn't there in front of us—animals can't do that.'

He nodded. 'And why is it just about everyone can recognise a musical octave?' he said.

'You find it interesting, too.' She was pleased.

'What did your father die of?' he asked.

Billie swallowed hard. Sudden grief overwhelmed her. She struggled against tears.

'I'm really sorry,' Luke said. 'I didn't mean to upset you.'

'Not your fault,' she said. 'He lost his mind. One Sunday morning he went bathing in the Trinity River. He hated water, and he couldn't swim. I think he wanted to die. The coroner thought so too, but the jury took pity on us and called it an accident, so that we'd get the life insurance. It was a hundred dollars. We lived on that for about a year.' She took a deep breath. 'Let's talk about something else. Tell me about why you want to explore outer space.'

'I think it's the most exciting adventure mankind has ever had.'

'And I want to map the mind.' She smiled. 'We have something in common—big ideas.'

He laughed, then braked. 'Hey, we're coming to a fork in the road.'

She switched on the flashlight and looked at the map on her knee. 'You'll have to pull up, I can't find it.'

He stopped the car and leaned across to look at the map. 'Maybe we're here,' he said, pointing.

Instead of looking at the map, she found herself staring at his face. His hair fell forward over his left eye. Without thinking, Billie lifted her hand and stroked his cheek with the outside edge of her little finger. She saw bewilderment and desire in his eyes. 'Which way do we go?' she murmured.

He moved away suddenly and put the car in gear. 'We take . . .' He cleared his throat. 'We take the left fork. Why did you do that?'

'I don't know,' she said. 'I didn't intend to, it just happened.'

He took a bend too fast. 'I don't want to feel like this about you,' he said.

She was suddenly breathless. 'Like what?'

'Never mind.'

'We're here,' Billie said. They stopped outside a neat one-storey frame house with gingerbread eaves. 'Come in. Denny will make some coffee to keep you awake on the return trip.'

'No, thanks,' he said. 'I'll just wait here until you're safely inside.'

'You've been very kind to me.' She held out her hand to shake.

'Are we friends?' he said, taking her hand.

She lifted his hand to her face, kissed it, and pressed it against her cheek, closing her eyes. After a moment he moved his hand behind her head, pulled her to him, and they kissed. She held the lapel of his rough tweed coat and pulled him closer. Then she heard Denny's voice. 'Who's out there?'

She pulled away from Luke and looked out. There were lights on in the house, and Denny stood in the doorway, wearing a purple silk dressing gown.

She turned back to Luke. 'I could fall in love with you in about twenty minutes, but I don't think we can be friends.' She took a deep breath, and got out of the car.

'Billie?' said Denny. 'What are you doing here?'

She crossed the yard, stepped on to the porch and fell into his arms. 'Oh, Denny, I love that man, and he belongs to someone else.'

She heard the car move, and turned to wave. As it swung by, she saw Luke's face, and the glint of something shiny on his cheeks.

Then he disappeared into the darkness.

8.30AM: SIX AGENTS were gathered in Anthony Carroll's office, a large, bare room with cheap wartime furniture. Anthony liked the spartan look.

Secret agents in America had never been as powerful as they were in January 1958. The Director of the CIA, Allen Dulles, was the brother of John Foster Dulles, Eisenhower's Secretary of State. The CIA's Plans Directorate—also known as CS, for Clandestine Services—had carried out coups against left-leaning governments in Iran and Guatemala, and the White House had been delighted at how cheap and bloodless these were by comparison with the war in Korea.

Within the Plans Directorate was Technical Services, the division that Anthony headed. The fact that the CIA was prohibited, by law, from operating within the United States was no more than a minor inconvenience to Technical Services. Theoretically it was a training division, but 'training' served as an all-purpose cover for covert actions inside the USA. Just about anything Anthony wanted to do, from bugging the phones of union bosses to testing truth drugs on prison inmates, could be labelled a training exercise. The surveillance of Luke was no exception.

Pete Maxell passed around a mugshot of Luke while Anthony briefed the agents: 'Our target today is a middle-ranking State Department employee with a high security clearance. He's having some kind of nervous breakdown. He flew in from Paris on Monday, spent Monday night in the Carlton Hotel, and went on a drinking binge on Tuesday. He stayed out all last night and went to a shelter for homeless people this morning. The security risk is obvious.'

Anthony's office door opened, and Carl Hobart came in. A

plump, bald man with spectacles, he was Anthony's immediate boss. Anthony groaned inwardly and continued with his briefing. 'But before we tip our hand, we want to see what the subject does, where he goes—who he contacts. A case like this, he may just be having trouble with his wife. But it could be that he's giving information to the other side, and now the strain has gotten to be too much for him. If he's involved in some kind of treason, we need all the information we can get before we pick him up.'

Hobart interrupted. 'What's this?'

Anthony turned to him slowly. 'A little exercise. We're conducting surveillance on a suspect diplomat.'

'Give it to the FBI,' Hobart said. 'It's the their job, not ours.'

'A case like this can unlock a horde of information if we handle it right, but the Feds are only interested in getting publicity for putting Reds in the electric chair. Anyway, when was the last time the FBI gave us anything?'

'The last time was never,' Hobart said. 'But I've got another assignment for you. The White House has called for a report on ways to deal with a rebel group in Cuba. There's a top level meeting later this morning. I need you and all your experienced people to brief me.'

'You're asking me for a briefing on Fidel Castro?'

'Of course not. I know all about Castro. What I need from you are practical ideas for dealing with insurgency.'

Anthony despised this kind of mealy-mouthed talk. 'Why don't you say what you mean? You want to know how to take them out.'

'Maybe.'

Anthony laughed scornfully. 'Well, what else would we do—start a Sunday School for them?'

'That's for the White House to decide. Our job is to present options. You can give me some suggestions.'

Anthony was worried. He had no time for distractions today, and he needed all his best people to keep an eye on Luke. 'I'll see what I can do,' he said.

'My conference room, with all your most experienced agents, at ten o'clock—and no excuses.' He turned away.

Anthony made a decision. 'Watch my lips,' he said.

Reluctantly, Hobart stared at Anthony's face.

Enunciating carefully, Anthony said, 'No.'

Hobart's bald head reddened. 'You'll hear more about this,' he said. 'A lot more.' He went out and slammed the door.

'Back to work,' Anthony said. 'Now Simons and Betts are with the subject at this moment, but they're due to be relieved in a few minutes by Rifenberg and Horwitz. We'll run four shifts of six hours each, with a back-up team always on call. That's all for now.'

The agents trooped out. Anthony stayed at his desk, trying to be patient. Office politics infuriated him. After five minutes the phone rang and he picked it up. 'Carroll here.'

'You've been upsetting Carl Hobart again.' It was George Cooperman, Deputy Chief of Operations and a wartime comrade of Anthony's. He was Hobart's immediate superior. 'Get yourself over here.'

'Coming.' Anthony hung up. He opened his desk drawer and took out an envelope. Then he put on his coat and walked to Cooperman's office, which was in P Building, next door.

Cooperman was a tall, gaunt man of fifty. He was reading the Moscow newspaper *Pravda*. He threw it down and growled, 'What's your excuse this time?'

Anthony tossed the envelope on to the desk. Cooperman looked inside. 'Blueprints,' he said. 'Of a rocket. So what?'

'I took them from the surveillance subject. He's a spy.'

'And you chose not to tell Hobart that.'

'I want to follow this guy around until he reveals his whole network. Hobart would hand the case over to the FBI, who would throw him in jail, and his network would fade to black.'

'You're right. Still, I need you at this meeting. I'm chairing it. But you can let your team carry on the surveillance. If anything happens they can get you out of the conference room.'

'Thanks, George.'

Anthony got up to leave. Cooperman said, 'And make damn sure you run this surveillance right. If you screw up on top of insulting your boss, I may not be able to protect you.'

Back in his office, Anthony found Pete with the team that had been shadowing Luke: Simons, in a navy topcoat, and Betts wearing a green raincoat. Also there were the team that should have relieved them. 'What the hell is this?' Anthony said. 'Who's with Luke?'

Simons was carrying a grey Homburg hat, which shook as his hand trembled. 'Nobody,' he said.

'What happened?' Anthony roared. 'What happened?'

Pete answered. 'We, uh . . .' He swallowed. 'We've lost him.'

Part Two

10.00am: The Georgetown Mind Hospital was a redbrick Victorian mansion with a modern extension at the back. Billie Josephson parked her red Thunderbird and hurried into the building.

She hated to arrive this late. It seemed disrespectful of her work and her colleagues. She was late because of her mother. Billie had gone to get the heart pills and returned home to find Becky-Ma lying on her bed, fully dressed, gasping for breath. The doctor had come, but he had nothing new to say. Becky-Ma had a weak heart. If she felt breathless, she should lie down. She must remember to take her pills. Stress was bad for her. Billie resolved anew to walk on eggshells around her mother.

She stopped by the admissions office and glanced at the overnight register. A new patient had been brought in late yesterday, after she had left: Joseph Bellow, a schizophrenic. Surprisingly, the patient had been discharged during the night. That was odd.

She passed through the day room on the way to her office. The subjects of Billie's research sat around, some watching TV or playing games, a few gazing vacantly into space. She waved to Tom, a young man with aphasia. 'How are you, Tommy?' she called. He grinned and waved back. He could read body language well, and often responded as if he knew what people were saying, so it had taken Billie months to figure out that he did not understand a single word.

Through the glass wall of an interview room she saw Ronald, a brilliant architect who had suffered head injuries in a car crash. He could look at a group of objects on a tray and say whether there were three or four of them, but if there were twelve and he had to count them, he had trouble. This suggested to Billie that the ability to see at a glance how many items are in a small group is a separate skill from the ability to count.

In this way, she was slowly charting the depths of the mind, locating memory here, language there, mathematics somewhere else. If the disability was related to brain damage, she could speculate that the normal ability was located in the damaged part of the brain. Eventually, her conceptual picture of the mind's functions would be mapped onto a physical diagram of the human brain. At her present rate of progress, it would take about two hundred years. With a team of psychologists she could progress much faster. She might see the map completed in her lifetime. That was her ambition.

She went up the stairs, thinking about the mystery patient, Joseph Bellow. Why had he been discharged in the middle of the night?

She reached her office and looked out of the window onto a building site. A new wing was being added to the hospital—and a new post was to be created to go with it: Director of Research. Billie had applied for the job, but so had one of her colleagues, Dr Leonard Ross. Len was older, but Billie had wider experience and had published more. She wanted the job badly.

On the building site she noticed, among the workmen, a small group of men in business clothes. Looking more closely, she saw that Len Ross was with them.

She spoke to her secretary. 'Who are those guys being shown around by Len Ross?'

'They're from the Sowerby Foundation.'

The Foundation was financing the new post. They would have a big say in who got the job. 'Did we know they were coming?'

'Len said he had sent you a note. He came by this morning, but you weren't here.'

There had never been a note, Billie felt sure. Len had deliberately failed to warn her. And she had been late. 'Damn,' Billie said. She rushed out to join the party on the building site.

She did not think about Joseph Bellow again for several hours.

11.00AM: AS LUKE NEGOTIATED the grid of streets leading to Union Station, he found himself checking, every minute or two, to see whether he was being followed. He had lost his shadows more than an hour ago, but they might now be searching for him. The thought made him fearful and bewildered. Who were they and what were they doing? He had to find out.

But first he had to clean himself up. His plan was to steal a suitcase from a train passenger. It would not be easy. His dirty, ragged clothing would stand out in a crowd of respectable travellers. If he were arrested, the police would never believe he was anything but a deadbeat. He would end up in jail. It was not prison itself that scared him, so much as the prospect of weeks or months of ignorance and confusion, not knowing who he was and helpless to find out.

Thinking ahead, he figured that after the theft he would have to disappear fast. He needed a car. The knowledge of how to steal one came to his mind immediately.

Close to the station, the street was lined with parked cars. He slowed his pace as a car pulled into a slot ahead of him. It was a blue and white Buick, new but not ostentatious. It would do fine. The starter would be operated with a key, not a handle, but it would be easy to pull out a couple of wires behind the dash and bypass the ignition. He wondered how he knew that.

A man in a dark topcoat got out of the Buick, took a briefcase from the trunk, locked the car, and headed for the station.

Luke waited until there was no one around, then he walked to the driver's door. Pressing his hands flat against the glass of the window, he pushed down. Nothing happened. He stood on tiptoe, to add the weight of his body to the pressure on the window mechanism. At last the pane of glass slid slowly down. When the window was fully open, he reached in and unlocked the door. He opened it, wound up the window, and closed the door. Now he was ready for a fast getaway.

He considered starting the car and leaving the engine running, but that might draw the attention of a passing patrolman.

He returned to Union Station. The best time to steal a suitcase would be immediately after the arrival of a large, crowded train.

when the concourse was thronged with hurrying people. He studied the information board. An express from New York was due in a few minutes. He hurried to the gate and waited.

As the passengers emerged, he watched them intently. He was looking for a man his own size and build.

At least a hundred passengers came out before Luke saw his mark. He was Luke's height, build and age. His grey topcoat was unbuttoned to show a tweed sports jacket and flannel pants—which meant he probably had a business suit in the tan leather suitcase he carried.

Luke shoved his way through the crowd until he was directly behind the man. Then he tripped him.

The man cried out and fell forward. He let go of both briefcase and suitcase, and crashed into a woman in a fur coat. She, too, stumbled, giving a little scream, and fell to the ground. While other passengers gathered around, trying to help, Luke calmly picked up the tan suitcase and walked away.

At the exit, he glanced back. A tall man was scanning the concourse, as if looking for something. His head swivelled suddenly towards Luke. Luke stepped quickly through the door.

Outside, he walked to the Buick. He looked back towards the station. The tall man was running across the traffic circle in front of the station, heading Luke's way.

Luke opened the driver's door and slung the bag onto the back seat. Then he got in and slammed the door. He reached under the dash and found the wires on either side of the ignition lock. He pulled them out and touched them together. Nothing happened. There was another wire to the right of the ignition. He pulled it out and touched it to the wire on the left.

The engine started. He put the transmission into drive, released the parking brake, and pulled out. Then he drove off.

A smile crossed his face. Unless he was very unlucky, he had a complete set of fresh clothes in the bag. He felt he had begun to take charge of his life. Now he needed somewhere to shower and change

12 NOON: THE COUNTDOWN stood at X minus 630 minutes, and Cape Canaveral was buzzing. The Explorer team had built and launched many missiles, but this would be the first of them to break free of the Earth's pull and fly beyond the atmosphere. For most of the team, tonight's launch would be the fulfilment of a lifetime's hopes. Elspeth felt the same way.

They were based in Hangar D and Hangar R, which were side by side. Elspeth was in Hangar R. She had a desk in the office of her boss, Willy Fredrickson, the launch conductor. Her job was to prepare and distribute the launch timetable.

Trouble was, the timetable changed constantly. Nobody in America had sent a rocket into space before. New problems arose all the time, and the engineers were forever improvising ways to jury-rig a component. Here, duct tape was called missile tape. So Elspeth produced regular updates of the timetable and distributed them. The job required her to go everywhere and know almost everything. Her title was secretary, and she was paid a secretary's wages, but no one could have done the job without a science degree.

She set out to distribute her noon update. She was rushed off her feet today, but that suited her: it stopped her worrying constantly about Luke and phoning Anthony every four minutes. She went first to the press department. The missile men had learned, from bitter experience, that a routine postponement could be made to look like a failure when the newspapers reported it. So they had a deal with all the major news organisations. They gave advance notification of launches only on condition that nothing would be published until there was 'fire in the tail', which meant the rocket engine had been ignited.

It was an all-male office, and several men stared at Elspeth as she walked across the pressroom. She knew she was attractive, but there was something formidable about her that made men who were inclined to whistle, or call her 'Honeybunch', think again.

In the Missile Firing Laboratory she found five shirtsleeved scientists at a bench, staring worriedly at a flat piece of metal that looked as if it had been in a fire. The group leader, Dr Keller, said, 'Good afternoon, Elspeth.' He spoke in heavily accented English. Like most of the scientists, he was a German who had been captured at the end of the war and brought to America to work on the missile programme.

She handed him a copy of her update and he took it. Elspeth nodded at the object on the table and said, 'What's that?'

'A jet vane. The burning fuel erodes the metal,' he explained. 'This always happens, to some extent. But with normal alcohol fuel the vanes last long enough to do their job. Today we are using a new fuel, which has a longer burning time, but it may erode the vanes so much that they become ineffective for steering. We have not had time to run sufficiently many tests on it.'

'Is this is going to delay the launch?' she asked. She felt she could not stand a postponement. The suspense was already killing her.

'That's what we're trying to decide. I think our answer is going to be: Let's take the chance.' The others nodded gloomily.

'I'll keep my fingers crossed,' Elspeth said.

She went outside into the scorching Florida sun, crossed a dusty apron and entered Hangar D. In the telemetry room she saw Hans Mueller, known as Hank. He pointed a finger at her and said, 'One hundred thirty-five.'

It was a game they played. She had to say what was unusual about the number. 'Too easy,' she said. 'Take the first digit, add the square of the second, plus the cube of the third, and you get the number you first thought of.'

'Correct! You win the big prize.' He fished a dime out of his pocket.

She took it. 'I'll give you a chance to win it back,' she said. 'One hundred thirty-six.'

'Ah.' He frowned. 'Wait. Sum the cubes of its digits and you get two hundred forty-four. Repeat the process, and you get the number you first thought of.'

She gave him back his dime, and a copy of her update.

She found Willy Fredrickson in the communications room with two army technicians. The teletype machine was not working and Willy was frustrated. But he gave her a grateful look as he took the update, and said, 'Elspeth, you are twenty-two carat gold.'

A moment later, two men approached Willy: a young army officer carrying a chart, and Stimmens, one of the scientists. The officer said, 'We got a problem.' He handed Willy the chart. 'The jet stream has moved south, and it's blowing at one forty-six knots.'

Elspeth's heart sank. The jet stream was a wind in the

stratosphere between 30,000 and 40,000 feet. It did not normally extend over Cape Canaveral, but it could move. And if it was too fierce, it might throw the missile off course.

Willy turned to Stimmens. 'We've allowed for this, haven't we?'

'Not really,' Stimmens said. 'We figure the missile can withstand winds up to one twenty knots, no higher.'

Willy turned back to the officer. 'What's the forecast for tonight?'

'Up to one seventy-seven knots.'

Willy ran a hand over his head. Elspeth knew what he was thinking. The launch might have to be postponed. 'Send up a weather balloon,' he ordered. 'We'll review the forecast again at five o'clock.'

Elspeth made a note to add the meeting to her timetable, then she left, feeling despondent. They could solve engineering problems, but there was nothing they could do about the weather.

Outside, she got into a Jeep and drove to Launch Complex 26. She pulled up outside the blockhouse and looked across to Launch Pad 26B. The gantry was a derrick from an oil rig, adapted for this purpose and coated with orange rust-resistant paint to protect it from corrosion by the humid, salty Florida air. The long white pencil of the Jupiter-C rocket seemed caught in the tangle of orange girders like a dragonfly in a spider's web. The men called it 'she', despite its phallic shape, and Elspeth, too, thought of the rocket as female. A bridal veil of canvas had concealed the upper stages from prying eyes since it arrived here, but that had now been removed, and the missile stood fully revealed, sunshine gleaming off its spotless paintwork.

The scientists knew that the eyes of the world were on them. Four months ago, the Soviet Union had stunned the world by sending up the world's first space satellite, the Sputnik. A month later they had sent up a second satellite, Sputnik 2, with a dog on board. Americans were devastated. A dog today, a man tomorrow.

President Eisenhower promised an American satellite before the end of the year. Early in December the US Navy launched the Vanguard rocket. It rose a few feet, burst into flames, toppled sideways and smashed to pieces. IT'S A FLOPNIK! said one headline.

The Jupiter-C was America's last hope. There was no third rocket. If this failed today, the United States was out of the space race. The American space programme would be in total disarray, and the USSR would control outer space for the foreseeable future.

All that, Elspeth thought, resting on this one rocket.

Vehicles were banned from the launch-pad area, except for essential ones such as fuel trucks, so she left her car and walked across the open space. At the back of the derrick was a long steel cabin containing offices and machinery. Elspeth entered by a metal door.

The gantry supervisor, Harry Lane, sat on a folding chair studying a blueprint. 'Hi, Harry,' she said brightly.

He grunted. He did not like to see women around the launch pad, and no sense of courtesy constrained him from letting her know it.

She dropped an update on a metal table and left. Driving back to the hangar, she realised she had a perfect excuse for calling Anthony. She would tell him about the jet stream, then ask about Luke.

In her office she dialled Anthony's direct line and got him right away. 'The launch is likely to be postponed until tomorrow. There are strong winds in the stratosphere.'

'I didn't know there were winds up there.'

'There's one. It's called the jet stream. The postponement isn't definite; there's a weather review meeting at five. How's Luke?'

'Well, we have a problem there. We've lost him.'

Elspeth's heart missed a beat. 'What?'

'He slipped away from my men.'

'God help us,' she said. 'Now we're in trouble.'

1941: IT WAS DAWN when Luke got back to Cambridge House and climbed the stairs to his room. He fell into bed in his underwear. The next thing he knew, Anthony was shaking him, saying, 'Get up.'

He opened his eyes. 'What's the time?' he mumbled.

'It's one o'clock, and Elspeth is waiting for you downstairs.'

The mention of Elspeth's name jogged his memory. He did not love her any more. He had fallen in love with Billie. It would make a train wreck of all their lives: his own, Elspeth's, Billie's and Anthony's.

Luke got up and pulled on a pair of flannels, a sweater and tennis shoes, and staggered downstairs.

Elspeth was waiting in the lobby, the only part of the building where girls were allowed. It was a spacious hall with a fireplace and comfortable chairs. She was as eye-catching as ever, in a wool dress the colour of bluebells, and a big hat. She laughed when she saw him. 'You look like a small boy who can't wake up!'

He kissed her cheek and slumped into a chair. 'It took hours to get to Newport,' he said.

'You've obviously forgotten you're supposed to take me to lunch,' Elspeth said brightly.

He looked at her. She was beautiful but he did not love her. He felt he was the worst kind of heel.

'Can we skip lunch? I haven't even shaved.'

A troubled shadow crossed her face, and he realised that she knew perfectly well something was wrong. But her reply was care-free. 'Of course,' she said.

'I'm sorry you got dressed up for nothing,' he said miserably.

'It wasn't for nothing—I saw you. And your fellow housemen seemed to like my outfit.' She stood up. 'Anyway, Professor and Mrs Durkham are having a party. I'll go there.'

Luke stood and helped her into her coat. 'We could meet later. He had to tell her today—it would be deceitful to let any more time pass without revealing the truth.'

'That'll be fine,' she said gaily. 'Pick me up at six.'

Luke returned woefully to his room. 'Has anyone said anything about last night?' he asked Anthony.

'Not a thing.'

'Billie's quite a gal,' Luke said.

'Isn't she great?' Anthony said. Luke observed with dismay the look of pride on his room-mate's face. To steal someone else's girlfriend was despicable in any circumstances, but the fact that Anthony was obviously crazy about Billie made every-thing even worse.

Luke groaned, and Anthony said, 'What's the matter?'

'I'm not in love with Elspeth any more. I think I have to end it. I feel like a heel.'

Anthony looked shocked. 'That's too bad. You two are quite an item. Have you proposed?'

'No, but we've talked about how many children we'll have.'

'You're still not engaged.'

'I guess you're right, but all the same I feel like a heel.'

There was a tap at the door, and a man Luke had never seen before came in. He was carrying two envelopes.

'The Dean of Students has asked me to hand you these notes in person.' He gave them an envelope each and left.

Anthony ripped open his envelope. 'Damn it.'

Luke opened his and read the short note inside asking him to come to the Dean's study at three o'clock that afternoon. Such letters always meant disciplinary trouble. Someone had reported to Dean Ryder that there had been a girl in the House last night. Anthony would probably be expelled.

There was another knock at the door, and in came Geoff Pidgeon, the amiable, chubby occupant of the room opposite. 'Didn't I just see the Dean's clerk?'

Luke waved his letter. 'Too damn right.'

'You know,' Geoff said to Anthony, 'I haven't said a word to anyone about seeing you with that girl.

'But who did? The only sneak in the House is Jenkins and he's away for the weekend.'

'No, he's not,' Pidgeon said. 'He changed his plans.'

'Then it's him,' Anthony said. 'I'm going to strangle that son of a bitch with my own hands.'

'I wonder if Elspeth and Billie have had letters,' Luke said.

Pidgeon said, 'If Jenkins knows their names, we can be sure he reported them.'

'Elspeth is safe,' Luke said. 'She wasn't here. But Billie could be expelled. Then she'll lose her scholarship. She explained it to me last night. She won't be able to study anywhere else.'

'I can't worry about Billie now,' Anthony said. 'I have to figure out what I'm going to do.'

Luke was shocked. Anthony had got Billie into trouble, and by Luke's code he should be more worried about her than about himself. But Luke saw an pretext to talk to Billie, and he could not resist it. Suppressing a guilty feeling, he said, 'Why don't I go to the girls' dorm and see whether Billie's back from Newport yet?'

'Would you?' Anthony said. 'Thanks.'

Luke shaved and changed his clothes. It was two o'clock when he reached the Radcliffe dormitory. A uniformed maid let him into the lobby. He asked for Billie. The maid sat at a desk, picked up a speaking-tube of the kind used on ships, blew into the mouthpiece, and said, 'Visitor for Miss Josephson.'

Billie came down wearing a dove-grey cashmere sweater and a plaid skirt. She looked lovely but distraught. She and Elspeth had been summoned to the office of Peter Ryder.

She showed him into the smoking room, where girls were allowed to receive male visitors. 'What am I going to do?' she said. Her face was drawn with distress, but Luke found her even more ravishing than yesterday.

'Anthony could say it was someone else in the room.'

Billie shook her head. 'They wouldn't believe it.' With a bitter smile, she said, 'I'll have to go back to Dallas and be a secretary to an oil man in cowboy boots.'

Two girls burst into the lounge, their faces flushed. 'Have you heard the news?' said one.

Luke shook his head, and Billie said desultorily, 'What's happened?'

'We're at war! The Japanese have bombed Hawaii!'

Luke could hardly take it in. 'Hawaii? What the heck for?'

'Is this true?' asked Billie.

'Everyone's talking about it on the street. People are stopping their cars.'

Two more girls rushed in, talking excitedly. Someone brought a radio downstairs and plugged it in. When it had warmed up they heard an announcer's voice. 'The battleship *Arizona* is reported destroyed and the *Oklahoma* sunk in Pearl Harbor. First reports say that more than one hundred US aircraft were crippled on the ground. American casualties are estimated to be at least two thousand dead and a thousand more injured. No warning was given for the Japanese attack.'

Billie said, 'It means war, doesn't it?'

'You bet it does,' Luke said angrily.

She squeezed his hand. 'I don't want you to be in a war,' she said. There were tears in her eyes. 'I don't want you hurt.'

'I'm so happy you feel that way.' He smiled ruefully. 'The world is falling apart, and I'm happy.' He looked at his watch. 'I suppose we all have to see the Dean, even though we're at war.' Then he was struck by a thought. 'Maybe there is a way for you and Anthony to stay at Harvard.'

ELSPETH WAS NERVOUS when the four of them met outside the Dean's study, but she told herself that she did not need to be afraid. She had broken the curfew last night, but she had not been caught. Anthony and Billie were the ones who were in trouble.

The Dean summoned them inside. He was a fussy, old-fashioned man in a neat suit of black coat and waistcoat with grey pants. His bow tie was a perfect butterfly, and his oiled hair looked like black paint on a boiled egg. With him was a grey-haired spinster called Iris Rayford who was responsible for the moral welfare of Radcliffe girls.

They sat in a circle of chairs, as if for a tutorial. The Dean lit a cigarette. 'Now, you boys had better tell the truth,' Dean Ryder said. 'What happened in your room last night?'

Anthony ignored Ryder's question and acted as if he were in charge of the proceedings.

'Where's Jenkins?' he said curtly. 'He's the sneak, isn't he? A man has a right to be confronted by his accuser.'

'This isn't a court, Mr Carroll,' the Dean said. 'Miss Rayford and I have been asked to establish the facts. Disciplinary proceedings, if necessary, will follow in due course.'

'Enough of this,' Luke said with an impatient gesture. 'I brought a woman into the House last night, sir.'

The Dean frowned. 'My information is that it was Mr Carroll who invited the woman in.'

'I'm afraid you've been misinformed.'

Anthony said, 'Luke, I don't know what you're doing, but—'

'Let me tell the story,' Luke said. 'I met the girl at the Dew Drop Inn, a waitress there. Her name is Angela Carlotti.'

The Dean said, 'I was told that the person seen in Cambridge House was Miss Bilhah Josephson here.'

'No, sir,' Luke said. 'Miss Josephson is a friend of ours, but she spent last night at the home of a relative in Newport.'

Miss Rayford spoke to Billie. 'Will the relative confirm that?'

Billie shot a bewildered look at Luke, then said, 'Yes.'

Ryder said to Luke, 'Can you produce this . . . waitress?'

'Yes, sir, I can. But I don't intend to bring her into this.'

'In that case, you make it difficult for me to accept your story.'

'I don't think Miss Carlotti's evidence will be necessary.'

'I beg to differ, Mr Lucas.'

Then Luke dropped his bombshell. 'I'm leaving the college tonight, sir. I'm going to join the army tomorrow.'

Elspeth cried, 'No!'

For the first time the Dean did not have an answer. He stared at Luke with his mouth open. Elspeth realised Luke had been clever. The college could hardly pursue a disciplinary action against a boy who was risking his life for his country. And if there were no investigation, then Billie was safe. A mist of grief obscured her vision. Luke had sacrificed everything—to save Billie.

Ryder was muttering about making his report and leaving others to decide. Miss Rayford wrote down the address of Billie's cousin. But it was all camouflage. They had been outwitted, and they knew it. At last the students were dismissed.

As soon as the door closed, Billie burst into tears. 'Don't go to war, Luke,' she said.

'You saved my life,' Anthony said. 'I'll never forget this.'

Luke turned to Elspeth. When he met her eye he flinched and she realised that her rage must be plainly visible. But she did not care. She stared at him for a moment then she raised her hand and slapped his face, once, very hard.

'You bastard,' she said. Then she turned and walked away.

1.00PM: LUKE WAS LOOKING for a quiet residential street. Driving away from Union Station he headed west. He crossed a river and found himself in a charming suburb of narrow streets lined with trees. He passed a building with a sign that read GEORGETOWN MIND HOSPITAL, and turned into a street of modest houses, which dead-ended in a cemetery. He parked the stolen Buick facing the way he had come, in case he had to make a fast getaway.

He needed some simple tools: a chisel or screwdriver and a hammer. There was probably a tool kit in the trunk—but the trunk was locked. It took him about thirty seconds to pick the lock. As he had hoped, there were a few tools in a box next to the jack. He chose the largest screwdriver. There was no hammer, but there was a heavy wrench that would serve. He put them in the pocket of his raincoat.

He took the stolen suitcase from the car and walked around the corner. He knew he was conspicuous, a ragged bum walking in a nice neighbourhood. If the local busybody called the cops, he could be in trouble. On the other hand, if all went well he might be washed and shaved and dressed like a respectable citizen in half an hour's time.

He drew level with the first house in the street, crossed a small front yard and knocked at the door.

ROSEMARY SIMS saw a nice blue and white car drive slowly past her house, and she wondered whose it was. She had good eyesight still, and she could watch most of the street from her comfy chair by the first-floor window. So she saw the stranger when he came walking around the corner. 'Strange' was the word. He wore no hat, his raincoat was torn and his shoes were tied up with string.

He went to Mrs Britsky's door and knocked. Mrs Britsky—a widow, living alone—looked out of the window and waved him away with a peremptory gesture.

He went to the next house, apparently intending to work his way along the street. Young Jeannie Evans came to the door with baby Rita in her arms. She fished in the pocket of her apron and gave him something, probably a few coins. So he was a beggar.

Old Mr Clark came to the door in his bathrobe. The stranger got nothing out of him.

The owner of the next house, Mr Bonetti, was at work, and his pregnant wife had left five minutes ago, heading for the store. The stranger studied the door and glanced up and down the street.

Mrs Sims turned away from the window and lifted the handset of the phone beside her seat. Slowly she dialled the number of the local police station, which she knew by heart.

Luke had to act fast. He inserted the screwdriver between the door and the jamb at the level of the lock. Then he struck the handle with the wrench, trying to force the blade into the socket of the lock. The first blow failed. He wiggled the screwdriver and used the wrench again, hammering as hard as he could. The screwdriver sank in an inch. He pulled sideways on the handle. To his profound relief, the door opened inwards.

He stepped quickly inside and closed the door behind him.

WHEN ROSEMARY SIMS finished dialling the number, she looked out of the window again, but the stranger had vanished.

That was quick.

The police answered. Feeling confused, she hung up the phone without speaking.

IT WAS THE HOME of a young couple. They had a new couch and a big TV set in the living room, but they were still using orange crates for storage in the kitchen. An unopened letter on the hall radiator was addressed to Mr G. Bonetti.

Luke went upstairs. Of three bedrooms, only one was furnished. He threw the suitcase on the bed. Inside it he found a carefully folded blue stripe suit, a white shirt and a conservative striped tie. There were dark socks, clean underwear, and a pair of black wing-tip shoes that looked only about half a size too big.

He stripped off his filthy clothes and kicked them into a corner. It gave him an odd feeling, to be naked in the home of strangers. He thought of skipping the shower, but he smelt bad, even to himself.

He crossed the tiny landing to the bathroom. It felt great to stand under the hot water and soap himself all over. When he got out, he dried himself with a pink bath towel and put on undershorts, pants, socks and shoes from the stolen case.

Luke found a safety razor and a shaving brush. He lathered his face and shaved quickly. Mr Bonetti didn't have any cologne, but maybe there was some in the suitcase. After stinking like a pig all morning, he liked the idea of smelling sweet.

He found a neat leather toiletry case and unzipped it. No

cologne was inside—but there was a hundred dollars in twenties, neatly folded: emergency money. He pocketed the cash, resolving to pay the man back one day.

He put on the shirt, tie and jacket. They fitted well and were of good quality. There was a mirror on the bedroom door. He had not looked at his reflection since early this morning in the men's room at Union Station, when he had been so shocked to see a filthy hobo staring back at him. He stepped up to the mirror, bracing himself.

He saw a tall, fit-looking man in his middle thirties, with black hair and blue eyes. A weary sense of relief swept over him. Take a guy like that, he thought. What would you say he does for a living? His hands were soft and did not look like those of a manual worker. He had a smooth face, one that had not spent much time out in bad weather. His hair was well cut. The guy in the mirror looked comfortable in the clothes of a corporate executive.

There was no hat or coat in the bag. Luke knew he would be conspicuous without either, on a cold January day. He opened the closet. Mr Bonetti had a sports jacket and a black suit he probably wore to church. There was no topcoat, but there was a lightweight raincoat. Luke took it off the hanger and put it on. It was a size small, but wearable. There was no hat, just a tweed cap that was too small. Luke would have to buy a hat, but the cap would serve for an hour or so—

He heard a noise downstairs. He froze, listening.

A young woman's voice said, 'What happened to my front door?'

Another voice, similar, replied, 'Looks like someone tried to break in! Maybe you should call the cops.'

Luke cursed under his breath.

'I don't know . . . looks like the thieves didn't get in.'

'How do you know? Better check if anything's been stolen.'

Luke realised he had to get out of there fast. He opened the bedroom window. There was no convenient tree or drainpipe down which he could climb.

'I'm going to look upstairs. We'll look pretty silly if we call the cops and there's no one here.'

Luke heard footsteps on the stairs. He crossed the landing to the bathroom and stood behind the door.

The footsteps mounted the staircase, crossed the landing and entered the bedroom. A voice said, 'Whose bag is that?'

Luke slipped out of the bathroom and tiptoed down the stairs.

'What kind of burglar brings luggage?'

'I'm calling the cops right now. This is spooky.'

Luke opened the front door and stepped outside.

He smiled. He had done it.

MRS SIMS FROWNED, mystified. The man leaving the Bonetti house had on Mr Bonetti's black raincoat and his tweed cap, but he was larger than Mr Bonetti.

She watched him walk down the street and turn the corner. A minute later the blue and white car she had noticed earlier came around the corner, going too fast. She realised then that the man who had left the house was the beggar she had been watching. He must have broken in and stolen Mr Bonetti's clothes!

As the car passed her window, she read the licence plate and memorised the number.

2.00PM: IN A MENSWEAR store, Luke bought a grey felt hat and a navy wool topcoat. At last, he felt he could look the world in the eye.

Now he was ready to attack his problems. First he had to learn something about memory, what caused amnesia and how long it might last. Where did one go for information? A library. He got a street map of Washington at a newsstand. Prominently displayed was the Central Public Library, at the intersection of New York and Massachusetts Avenues. Luke drove there.

The effect of his new appearance was immediately apparent. The grey-haired librarian behind the counter stood up and said, 'Can I help you, sir?'

'I want to look at books on memory,' Luke said.

'That'll be the psychology section.' She led him up a grand staircase to the next floor and pointed to a corner.

Luke looked along the shelf. There were plenty of books on psychoanalysis, child development, and perception, none of which were any use. He picked out a fat tome called *The Human Brain* and browsed through it, but it seemed highly technical. There were some equations, and a certain amount of statistical material, which he found easy enough to understand.

Then his eye was caught by *An Introduction to the Psychology of Memory* by Bilhah Josephson. He pulled it out and found a chapter on disorders of the memory. He read: 'The common condition in which the patient "loses his memory" is known as "global amnesia".' Luke was elated. He was not the only person to whom this had happened.

> Such a patient does not know his identity and will not recognise his own parents or children. However, he remembers a great deal else. He may be able to drive a car, speak foreign languages, and name the Prime Minister of Canada. The condition would be more appropriately called 'autobiographical amnesia'.

This was exactly what had happened to him. He could still check whether he was being tailed and start a stolen car without the key.

Dr Josephson outlined her theory that the brain contained several different memory banks, like separate filing cabinets, for different kinds of information.

> The autobiographical memory records events we have experienced personally. The long-term semantic memory holds general knowledge such as the capital of Romania and how to solve quadratic equations. The short-term memory is where we keep a phone number for the few seconds in between looking it up in the phone book and dialling it.

She gave examples of patients who had lost one filing cabinet but retained others, as Luke had. He felt profound relief, and gratitude to the author of the book.

Then he was struck by an inspiration. He was in his thirties, so he must have followed some occupation for a decade. His professional knowledge should still be in his head, lodged in his long-term semantic memory. He ought to be able to use it to figure out his line of work. Thinking back over the last few minutes, he had noticed that he had easily understood the equations and statistics in *The Human Brain*. Maybe he was in a profession that involved numbers: perhaps an accountant or a maths teacher.

He found the maths section and looked along the shelves. A book called *Number Theory* caught his attention. He browsed through it. It was clearly presented, but some years out of date . . . Suddenly he looked up. He had discovered something. He understood number theory. And the book was not written for the curious layman. It was an academic work. He had to be some kind of scientist.

With mounting optimism, he located the chemistry shelf and picked out *Polymer Engineering*. He found it comprehensible but not easy. Next he moved to physics and tried *A Symposium on the Behaviour of Cold and Very Cold Gases*. It was fascinating, like reading a good novel.

His job involved maths and physics. What branch of physics? Cold gases were interesting, but he did not feel that he knew as much as the author of the book. He scanned the shelves and picked out *Principles of Rocket Design*. It was an elementary text, but nevertheless there was an error on the first page he looked at. Reading on, he found two more. 'Yes,' he said aloud, startling a nearby schoolboy who was studying a biology text. If he could recognise mistakes in a textbook, he had to be an expert. He was a rocket scientist.

He hurried to the information desk and asked, 'Is there any kind of list of scientists?'

'Sure,' the librarian said. '*The Dictionary of American Scientists*.'

He found the book easily. He sat and went through the index, searching for anyone named Luke. He found a biologist called Luke Parfitt, an archaeologist called Lucas Dimittry, and a pharmacologist called Luc Fontainebleu, but no physicist. Of course, he thought despondently, he was not even sure that Luke was his name. It was only what he had been called by Pete. For all he knew, his real name might be Percival.

He thought of another approach. Somewhere, there were people who knew him, friends and colleagues who would recognise him. Where did one find scientists? At a university.

He looked up Washington in the encyclopedia. The entry included a list of universities in the city. He picked Georgetown University because he had been in the Georgetown area earlier and knew how to get back there. On his street map, he saw that the university had a large campus. It would probably have a big physics department with dozens of professors. Surely one of them would know him?

Full of hope, he left the library and got back into his car.

2.30PM: WHEN THE CUBA MEETING took a coffee break, Anthony ran back to Q Building for an update from his team.

Pete met him on the stairs. 'Here's a weird report from the police in Georgetown,' he said. 'A housewife came back from the store to find that her home had been broken into and her shower used. The intruder had disappeared, leaving behind a pile of filthy old clothes.'

'At last—a break,' Anthony said. 'Give me the address.'

'You think this is our guy?'

'I'm sure of it! He's fed up with looking like a bum, so he's broken into an empty house, showered, shaved and put on some decent clothes. Come on, let's go. Grab some photos of Luke.'

Anthony left the building with Pete following, and they jumped into his old Cadillac. 'This may need delicate handling,' he said. 'We don't have a hundred men to chase up leads so my plan is to get the Washington Police Department working for us.'

He drove quickly to the address in the police report. It was a small home on a quiet street. A police cruiser was parked outside.

Before going into the house, Anthony studied the opposite side of the street, scrutinising the houses. After a moment he spotted what he was looking for: a face in an upstairs window, watching him. It was an elderly woman, who returned his stare with unabashed curiosity. She was just what he needed, a neighbourhood busybody.

They went to the house that had been broken into. He could see scratches and a little splintering on the door jamb where the lock had been forced. A neat job, he thought. That fitted Luke.

The door was opened by an attractive young woman who was expecting a baby. She took Anthony and Pete into her living room where two men were sitting on the couch, drinking coffee and smoking. One was a uniformed patrolman, the other a detective. An open suitcase was on the coffee table in front of them.

Anthony showed his identification to the cops, but he did not want Mrs Bonetti to know that the CIA was interested in the case, so he said, 'We're colleagues of these police officers.'

The detective was Lewis Hite. 'You know something about this?'

'We may have some information that will help, but first, I need to know what you've got.'

'We got a suitcase belongs to a guy named Rowley Anstruther, from New York. He breaks into Mrs Bonetti's house, takes a shower, and goes away, leaving his suitcase behind. Go figure!'

Anthony looked through the contents of the leather case. There were clean shirts and underwear, but no shoes, pants or jackets. 'Looks like Mr Anstruther arrived in Washington from New York today,' he said.

Mrs Bonetti said, 'How do you know that?'

'The bag contains clean underwear but no laundry,' Hite explained. 'So he probably hasn't yet spent a night away.'

Anthony said, 'I believe some old clothes were also left behind.'

The patrolman said, 'I got 'em.' He lifted a cardboard box from beside the couch.

Anthony recognised the rags Luke had been wearing. 'I don't believe Mr Anstruther came to this house,' he said. 'I think the bag was stolen from him this morning, probably at Union Station. We have a picture of the man we believe stole the suitcase and broke into this house.' Anthony nodded to Pete, who handed Hite a photograph. 'He's six foot one, hundred eighty pounds, athletic build, and may pretend to have lost his memory.'

'So what's the story?' Hite was intrigued. 'This guy wanted Anstruther's clothes and came here to change?'

'Something like that.'

'You think he's still in town?'

'Yes.' Anthony was not as sure as he pretended.

'I presume he's in a car?'

'Let's find out.' Anthony turned to Mrs Bonetti. 'What's the name of the white-haired lady who lives across the street, a couple of doors down?'

'Rosemary Sims. We call her Nosy Rosie.'

'Excellent.' He turned to the detective. 'Let's have a word with her.'

They crossed the street and knocked on Mrs Sims's door. She opened it instantly—she had been waiting in the hall. 'I saw him!' she said. 'He went in there looking like a bum, and came out dressed to the nines.'

Hite said, 'Did he have a car, Mrs Sims?'

'Yes, a nice blue and white model.'

'Did you happen to notice the licence plate?' Hite asked.

'Yes,' she said triumphantly. 'I wrote it down.'

3.00PM: LUKE DROVE slowly through the iron gates of Georgetown University. He parked in front of the main entrance, a triple-arched portico marked HEALY HALL. Inside, a receptionist told him the way to the physics department. Following her directions, he found a large laboratory with a group of men who were working with the components of a microwave spectrograph. Judging by their ages, Luke thought they were professors and graduate students. He approached them with an expectant look.

One of the older men asked, 'Can I help you?'

'I hope so,' Luke said. 'Is there a department of geophysics here?'

'Goodness, no,' he said. 'At this university, even physics is considered a minor subject.' The others laughed.

'What about astronomy?'

'Why, yes, of course. Our observatory is famous.'

His spirits lifted. 'Where is it?'

The man gave him directions.

On the flat roof of a small two-storey house was a large revolving observatory, its dome having a sliding roof section. Luke approached it with mounting anticipation.

Inside, the rooms were arranged around a massive central pillar that supported the enormous weight of the dome. Luke opened a door and found an attractive woman about his own age sitting behind a typewriter. 'Good morning,' he said. 'Is the professor in?'

'You mean Father Heyden?'

'Uh, yes.'

'And you are?'

'Um . . . he won't know me,' Luke said. 'That is he will know me, I hope, but not by name.'

The secretary raised her eyebrows, 'Still, you do have a name.'

'Luke. Professor Luke.'

'To which university are you attached, Professor Luke?'

'Look, I didn't come here to be cross-examined. Just tell Father Heyden that Professor Luke, the rocketry physicist, has dropped by and would like a word with him.'

'I'm afraid that won't be possible,' she said firmly.

Luke left the room, slamming the door. He was angry with himself more than with the secretary, who was only protecting her boss. He decided to look around. The building seemed to be deserted. He climbed a wooden stair on the second floor and entered the observatory. It, too, was empty. He stood admiring the large revolving telescope, wondering what he was going to do next.

The secretary came up the stairs. He prepared himself for a row, but instead she spoke sympathetically. 'You're in some kind of trouble, aren't you,' she said.

Her kindness brought a lump to his throat. 'It's very embarrassing,' he said. 'I've lost my memory. I know I'm in the rocketry field, and I was hoping to run into someone who might recognise me.'

'All the faculty are at a lecture on rocket fuels at the Smithsonian Institute.'

Luke felt a surge of hope. 'Where's the Smithsonian Institute?'

'It's downtown, right in the Mall, around 10th Street.'

'What time is the lecture?'

'It started at three.'

Luke checked his watch. It was three thirty. 'Thank you,' he said, and he ran down the stairs and out of the building.

3.30PM: BILLIE WAS FURIOUS with Len Ross for trying to ingratiate himself with the people from the Sowerby Foundation. She was still annoyed that afternoon when the hospital's chief executive asked her to come to his office.

Charles Silverton waved Billie to a chair and said, 'Did you speak to the people from the Sowerby Foundation this morning?'

'Yes. Len was showing them around, and I joined the party.'

'Do you think you could have said anything to offend them?'

'I don't think so. We just talked about the new wing.'

'You know, I really wanted you to get the job of Director of Research. Len Ross is a competent scientist, but you're exceptional.'

'The Foundation is backing Len for the job?'

He hesitated. 'I'm afraid they're insisting on it, as a condition of their grant.'

'The hell they are.' Billie was stunned.

'Do you know anyone connected with the Foundation?'

'One of my oldest friends, Anthony Carroll, is a trustee. He's my son's godfather.'

'Why is he on the board? What does he do for a living?'

'He works for the State Department, but his mother is very wealthy, and he's involved with several charities.'

'Does he have a grudge against you?'

Billie had been angry with Anthony after the catastrophe that led to Luke's leaving Harvard, and they never dated again. But she forgave him because of how he behaved towards Elspeth, who had gone into a decline. She had let her academic work slip, and was in danger of failing to graduate. It was Anthony who rescued her. They became close, though the relationship was a friendship rather than a romance. They studied together, and she caught up enough to pass. Anthony won back Billie's respect, and they had been friends ever since.

She told Charles, 'I got kind of mad at him, back in 1941, but we made it up long ago.'

'Maybe someone on the board admires Len's work.'

Billie considered. 'Len's approach is different from mine. He's a Freudian; he looks for psychoanalytical explanations.'

'So there might be a keen Freudian on the board who is against you. Why don't you ask your friend?'

'That's exactly what I'm going to do,' she said.

3.45PM: LUKE CHECKED his watch as he drove along K Street. He would be at the Smithsonian in about ten minutes. He should arrive as the talk was ending. Then he would find out who he was.

He turned right on 9th Street. A few moments later, he heard a police siren blip once. He looked in his rear-view mirror. A police cruiser was on his tail, lights flashing. There were two cops on the front seat. One pointed towards the kerb and mouthed, 'Pull over.'

Luke had almost made it. Could he have committed some minor traffic violation? If they asked for his driving licence he had no kind of identification and he was driving a stolen car.

Ahead of him on the one-way street was a truck. Without further thought, he pulled around the truck. The cops switched on their siren and followed.

Luke pulled in front of the truck, going fast. Acting on instinct now, he yanked the parking brake and spun the wheel hard to the right. The Buick went into a long skid. The truck swerved left to avoid it. Luke's car came to rest facing the wrong way. He stepped on the gas, heading against the traffic on the one-way street.

Cars veered wildly left and right to avoid a head-on collision. Luke swung right to miss a city bus, then clipped a station wagon. He made it to the next crossing and swung right on to a broad avenue. He raced two blocks, running red lights, then looked in his mirror. There was no sign of the police car.

He turned again, heading south now. It was four o'clock, and he was farther away from the Smithsonian than he had been five minutes ago. He stepped on the gas. His luck changed. All the lights were green. He hit seventy crossing Constitution Avenue, and he was in the park.

He saw the big dark-red building like a castle in a fairy tale. He stopped the car and checked his watch. It was five past four. The audience would be leaving. He cursed and jumped out.

He ran across the grass. The secretary had told him the lecture was in the Aircraft Building around the back. He followed a little path to the side of the building, and found an elaborate iron gateway leading to the museum's back entrance. To his right was what looked like an old aircraft hangar. He went inside.

He looked around. All kinds of aircraft were suspended from the ceiling: old biplanes, a wartime jet, even a hot-air balloon. He spoke to a guard. 'I'm here for the lecture on rocket fuels.'

'You're too late,' the man said. 'The lecture's over.'

'Where was it held? I might still catch the speaker.'

'Far end of the hall,' the man said.

Most of the audience had left the lecture theatre, and attendants were already stacking the metal chairs. But a small knot of eight or nine men remained in a corner, deep in discussion, surrounding a white-haired man who might have been the lecturer.

Luke walked up to the group. The white-haired man glanced at him, looked back to the others, then carried on. 'Nitromethane is almost impossible to handle. You can't ignore safety factors.'

'You can build safety into your procedures,' said a young man in a tweed suit.

The argument was a familiar one to Luke. A variety of rocket fuels had been tested, many more powerful than the standard combination of alcohol and liquid oxygen, but they had drawbacks.

A man with a southern accent said, 'What about unsymmetrical dimethylhydrazine? I hear they're testing that at the Jet Propulsion Laboratory in Pasadena.'

Luke suddenly said, 'It works, but it's deadly poison.'

They all turned to him. The white-haired man frowned, looking slightly annoyed, resenting the interruption from a stranger.

Then the young man in the tweed suit looked shocked and said, 'My God, what are you doing in Washington, Luke?'

Luke felt so happy he could have wept.

Part Three

4:15pm: Luke found he could not speak. The emotion of relief was so strong it seemed to constrict his throat. All day he had forced himself to be calm and rational, but now he was close to breaking point.

The other scientists resumed their conversation, oblivious to his distress, except for the young man, who said, 'Hey, are you OK?'

Luke nodded. After a moment, he managed to say, 'Could we talk?'

'Sure.' He led Luke into a small room with a couple of chairs, a desk and a phone. They sat down. 'What's going on?' said the man.

'I've lost my memory. I still remember my science—that's how I found my way to you guys—but I don't know anything about myself.'

Looking shocked, the young man said, 'Do you know who I am?'

Luke shook his head. 'I'm not even sure of my own name.'

'You're Dr Claude Lucas, but everyone calls you Luke. I'm Will McDermot.'

Luke closed his eyes, overwhelmed by relief and gratitude. 'Thank you, Will. Do you know where I live?'

'Huntsville, Alabama. You work for the Army Ballistic Missile Agency, based at Redstone Arsenal in Huntsville. You're a civilian, though. Your boss is Wernher von Braun.'

'I can't tell you how good it is to know this stuff.'

'I was surprised to see you because your team is about to launch a rocket that will put an American satellite in space for the first time. They're all down in Cape Canaveral.'

'Did I work on that?'

'Yeah. The Explorer. It's the most important launch in the history of the American space programme.'

'I ought to be there for the launch,' Luke said.

'Exactly . . . so do you have any idea why you're not?'

Luke shook his head. 'I woke up this morning in the men's room at Union Station. No idea how I got there.'

Will grinned. 'Sounds like you went to a great party last night.'

'Is that the kind of thing I do? Get so drunk I pass out?'

'I don't know you well enough to answer that. I'd be surprised, though. You know us scientists. Our idea of a party is to sit around drinking coffee and talking about our work.'

That sounded right to Luke. 'I'm going to call Cape Canaveral.'

'Great idea.' Will picked up the phone on the desk and handed the phone to Luke.

Luke got the number from information and dialled. 'This is Dr Lucas.' He felt inordinately pleased to be able to give his name. 'I'd like to speak to someone on the Explorer launch team.'

A moment later a voice said, 'Army security. Colonel Hide speaking.'

'This is Dr Lucas—'

'Luke! At last! Where the hell are you? We've been going crazy! We got Army Security looking for you, the FBI, even the CIA!'

'I'm in Washington. Listen, a strange thing has happened. I lost my memory. I've been wandering around town trying to figure out who I am. Finally I found some physicists who know me.'

'But that's extraordinary. How did it happen?'

'I was hoping you could tell me that, Colonel.'

'OK, well, I'll tell you what I know. Monday morning you took off, saying you had to go to Washington. You flew from Patrick Air Force base, near Cape Canaveral. Marigold made the reservations—'

'Who's Marigold?'

'Your secretary in Huntsville. She booked your usual suite at the Carlton Hotel in Washington.'

'Did I tell anyone the purpose of the trip?'

'Marigold made an appointment for you to see General Sherwood at the Pentagon yesterday—but you didn't keep the appointment.'

'Did I give a reason for wanting to see the general?'

'Apparently not. His area of responsibility is army security—but he's also a friend of your family's.'

'Is the launch going ahead tonight?'

'No, we've got weather problems. It's been postponed until tomorrow night at ten thirty.'

'Do I have friends here in Washington?'

'Sure. One of them's been calling me every hour. Bern Rothsten.' Hide read out a phone number.

Luke scribbled it on a scratch pad. 'I'll call him right away.'

'First you should talk to your wife.'

Luke froze. Wife, he thought. I have a wife. 'What's her name?'

'Elspeth,' Hide said. 'I'll transfer you to her. Hold the line.'

Luke had a nervous sensation in his stomach.

'Elspeth speaking. Luke, is that you?' She had a warm, low voice.

He said, 'Yes, this is Luke. I've lost my memory.'

'I've been so worried. Are you OK?'

He felt grateful for someone who cared how he was. 'I guess I am now,' he said. 'I spent the day trying to find out who I am.'

'Everyone's been looking for you. Where are you now?'

'At the Smithsonian, in the Aircraft Building.'

'Is someone taking care of you?'

'A fellow scientist has been helping me. And I have a number for Bern Rothsten.'

Elspeth said, 'You don't remember why you took off for Washington in such a hurry?'

'No. Obviously I didn't tell you.'

'You said it was better for me not to know. But I was frantic. I called an old friend of ours in Washington, Anthony Carroll. He's in the CIA. He called you at the Carlton Monday night, and arranged to meet him for breakfast on Tuesday morning—but you didn't show up. I'm going to call him now and tell him everything's all right.'

'Obviously something happened to me between Monday evening and Tuesday morning.'

'You ought to see a doctor, get yourself checked out.'

'I feel fine. But there's a lot I want to know. Do we have children?'

'No. We've been trying for a baby ever since we got married, which is four years ago, but we haven't succeeded.'

'Do we know why?'

'No, but we've been talking about adopting.'

'Are my parents alive?'

'Your mom is. She lives in New York. Your pa died five years ago.'

Luke felt a sudden wave of grief that seemed to come from nowhere. He had lost his memories of his father, and would never see him again. It seemed unbearably sad.

Elspeth went on, 'You have two brothers and a sister, all younger. Your baby sister Emily is your favourite. She lives in Baltimore.'

'Do you have phone numbers for them?'

'Of course. Hold on while I look them up.'

'I'd like to talk to them, I don't know why.' He heard a muffled sob at the other end of the line. 'Are you crying?'

Elspeth sniffed. 'I'm OK. Suddenly I felt so sorry for you,' she said tearfully. 'It must have been awful.'

'There were some bad moments.'

'Let me give you those numbers.' She read them out.

'I could go on asking you questions all day. Would you fly up here tonight?'

There was a moment of silence. 'My God, why?'

'To figure out this mystery with me. I could use some help—and companionship.'

'Luke, I can't leave Cape Canaveral now. We're about to launch the first American satellite, for heaven's sake! I can't let the team down at a moment like this.'

'I guess not.' He understood, but all the same he was hurt by her refusal. 'Who's Bern Rothsten?'

'He was at Harvard with you and Anthony Carroll.'

'He's been trying to reach me. Maybe he knows what this is about.'

'Call me later, won't you? I'll be at the Starlite Motel tonight.'

'OK.'

'Take care of yourself, Luke, please,' she said earnestly.

'I will, I promise.' He hung up.

He felt emotionally drained. Part of him wanted to go to his hotel and lie down. But he picked up the phone again and called Bern Rothsten. 'This is Luke Lucas,' he said.

'Luke, thank God! What the hell happened to you?'

'I don't really know anything except that I've lost my memory.'

'You lost your memory? Do you know how this happened.'

'No. I was hoping you might have a clue. Why have you been trying to reach me?'

'I was worried. You called me on Monday from Huntsville.'

'Huntsville? I thought I flew from Florida.'

'You did, but you stopped off in Huntsville because you had an errand to run. You said you were on your way here and would call me from the Carlton. But you never did.'

'Something happened to me on Monday night.'

'Yeah. Listen, Billie Josephson is an expert on memory.'

The name rang a bell. 'I think I came across her book in the library.'

'She's also my ex-wife, and an old friend of yours.' Bern gave Luke the number.

'I'm going to call her right away. Bern . . .'

'Yeah.'

'I lose my memory, and it turns out that an old friend of mine is a world expert on memory. Isn't that a hell of a coincidence?'

4.45PM: BILLIE HAD an hour-long interview with a patient, but she was distracted during it, thinking about the Sowerby Foundation and Anthony Carroll. When it was over, she called Anthony. 'What the hell is going on?' she said abruptly. 'I was passed over for the post of Director of Research here at the hospital. Len Ross got the job. Did you know that?'

'Yeah, I guess I did.'

'I thought I might lose to a highly qualified outsider—Sol Weinberg, from Princeton, or someone of that order. But everyone knows I'm better than Len.'

'Do they?'

'Anthony, come on! You know it yourself. So why didn't I get the job? The foundation is insisting on Len.'

'I guess they have the right.'

'You're part of the foundation. It's very unusual for a trust to interfere in this kind of decision. They normally leave it to the experts. You must know why they took this step.'

'Well, I don't. There hasn't been a meeting about it.'

'Charles was very definite.'

'Most likely the Director and one or two board members had a chat over a drink at the Cosmos Club. One of them has called Charles and given him the word.'

'Charles was shocked. He can't understand why they would do such a thing.'

'Maybe the Director doesn't approve of women earning high salaries when there are men like Ross trying to support a family.'

'For God's sake! I have a child and an elderly mother to take care of.'

'I didn't say it was logical. Listen, Billie, I have to go.'

She hung up and stared at the phone, trying to sort out her feelings. The conversation rang false to her. It was perfectly plausible that Anthony might not know about machinations among the other board members of the foundation. So why did she disbelieve him? Thinking back, she realised he had been evasive—which was not like him.

Anthony was lying.

WHEN ANTHONY hung up the phone, it rang again immediately. He picked it up and heard Elspeth say, 'I've been on hold for a quarter of an hour.'

'I was talking to Billie, she—'

'Never mind. I just spoke with Luke. He was at the Smithsonian, in the Aircraft Building, with a bunch of physicists.'

'I'm on my way.' Anthony dropped the phone and ran out of the door. Pete saw him and ran after him. They went down to the parking lot and jumped into Anthony's car.

The fact that Luke had spoken with Elspeth dismayed Anthony. Everything was coming unglued. But if he got to Luke, maybe he could hold things together.

It took them four minutes to drive to Independence Avenue and 10th Street. Inside the Aircraft Building, Anthony said, 'I'll go right, you go left.' He walked through the exhibits, scrutinising the faces of the men as they stared up at the aircraft suspended from the ceiling. At the far end of the building he met up with Pete, who made an empty-hands gesture.

The men's room and offices were checked and yielded nothing.

Anthony said, 'This is a catastrophe.'

Outside on Independence Avenue, Anthony saw two cops checking out a car parked on the other side of the road. Anthony went closer and saw that the car was a blue and white Buick with the same licence plate Nosy Rosie had given him.

'Did you just spot this car illegally parked?' he said to them.

'No, we saw a man driving it on 9th Street,' one cop said. 'But he got away from us. Few minutes later, we see the car parked here, but he's gone.'

Anthony took a business card out of his wallet. 'If you get a report of a car stolen near by, would you please call me at this number?'

The cop read the card and said, 'I'll do that, Mr Carroll.'

As Anthony and Pete returned to the yellow Cadillac, Pete said, 'What do you think he'll do now?'

'I don't know.'

Anthony was silent, thinking, while he drove to Q Building. Reaching his office, he said, 'I want you to go with two men to the Carlton Hotel. Take a room, then stake out the lobby. I'll join you there later.'

Anthony shut the door of the office. This really was a catastrophe. Now that Luke knew his identity, there was no telling what else he might find out. If he could find him, he could still patch things up.

But he would have to take drastic measures. It would no longer be enough to put Luke under surveillance. He had to solve the problem once and for all.

With a heavy heart, he went to the photograph of President Eisenhower that hung on the wall. He pulled on one side of the frame, and the picture swung out to reveal a safe. He dialled the combination, opened the door, and took out his gun.

It was a Walther P38 automatic. This was the handgun used by the German army in the Second World War. Anthony had been issued with it before he went to North Africa. He also had a silencer that had been specially designed to fit it. He took the silencer from the safe, fitted it over the barrel of the pistol, and screwed it tight. He put on a long camel-hair winter coat, single-breasted, with deep inside pockets. He placed the gun in the right-hand pocket.

He buttoned his coat and went out.

6.00PM: LUKE TOOK A TAXICAB to the Georgetown Mind Hospital and gave his name at the reception desk, saying he had an appointment with Dr Josephson.

She had been charming on the phone: concerned about him, intrigued to know that he had lost his memory, eager to see him as soon as she could. Now she came running down the stairs, a short woman in a white lab coat, with big brown eyes and a flushed expression of excitement. Luke could not help smiling at the sight of her.

'It's so great to see you,' she said, throwing her arms around him.

He felt an impulse to respond to her exuberance but, afraid that he might do something to cause offence, he froze, his hands in the air like the victim of a holdup.

'You don't remember what I'm like,' she said, laughing. 'Relax, I'm almost harmless.'

He let his arms fall around her shoulders. Her small body was soft and round under the lab coat.

'Come on, I'll show you my office.' She led him up the stairs.

Billie had a small room with a plain desk and a steel filing cabinet, but she had made it pretty with flowers and a splashy abstract painting in bright colours. She gave Luke coffee and opened a package of cookies, then asked him about his amnesia.

She made notes as he answered her questions. Luke had had no food for twelve hours, and he ate all the cookies. She smiled and said, 'Want some more? There's another pack.' He shook his head.

'Well, I have a pretty clear picture,' she said eventually. 'You have global amnesia, but otherwise you seem mentally healthy. I can't assess your physical state, but you look all right, just shook up.'

'Is there a cure for this type of amnesia?'

'No, there's not. The process is generally irreversible.'

That was a blow. Luke had hoped that everything might come back to him in a flash.

'Don't be downhearted,' Billie said. 'Sufferers are able to relearn what has been forgotten, so they can usually pick up the threads of their lives and live normally. You're going to be fine.'

Even while he was hearing horrible news, he found himself watching her with fascination, concentrating on her eyes, which seemed to glow with sympathy, then her expressive mouth, then the way the light from the desk lamp fell on her dark curls. He said, 'What might have caused the amnesia?'

'Brain damage is the first possibility to consider. However, there's no sign of injury.'

'So what else?'

'It can be brought on by prolonged stress, a sudden shock, or drugs. It's also a side effect of some treatments for schizophrenia involving a combination of electric shock and drugs.'

'Any way to tell which affected me?'

'Not conclusively. You need to find out what happened to you between Monday night and this morning. What's your next step?'

Luke stood up. 'I'm going to see Bern Rothsten. He may have some ideas.'

'I'll see you out.'

As they walked down the stairs, Luke asked, 'How long have you been divorced from Bern?'

'Five years. Long enough to become friends again.'

'This is a strange question, but—did you and I ever date?'

'Oh, boy,' said Billie. 'Did we ever.'

1943: ON THE DAY Italy surrendered, Billie bumped into Luke in the lobby of Q Building. At first she did not know him. She saw a thin man of about thirty and her eyes passed over him. Then he spoke. 'Billie? Don't you remember me?'

She knew the voice, of course, and it made her heart beat faster. But he was emaciated. His shirt collar was too large, and his jacket looked as if it were draped over a wire hanger. His eyes were the eyes of an old man. 'Luke,' she said. 'You look terrible!'

'Gee, thanks,' he said, with a tired smile. 'I've lost weight, I know. There's not a lot of food where I've been. What are you doing here?'

'A training course—maps, radio, firearms, unarmed combat.'

He grinned. 'You're not dressed for jujitsu.'

Billie still loved to dress stylishly, despite the war. She could not afford to buy the latest fashions on her army wages, but her father had taught all his children to sew. 'I'll take that as a compliment,' she said. 'Where have you been?'

'Do you have a minute to talk?'

'Of course.'

'Let's go outside.'

It was a warm September afternoon. They walked alongside the reflecting pool. 'How come you're in OSS?' Luke asked.

'Anthony Carroll fixed it,' she said. He's Bill Donovan's personal assistant now.' General 'Wild Bill' Donovan was head of OSS. 'He's brought in all his old friends from Harvard. Elspeth is in London, Peg is in Cairo, and I gather you and Bern have been behind enemy lines somewhere.'

'France,' Luke said.

'What was that like?'

'The first man I killed was a Frenchman,' he said abruptly. It was painfully obvious that he needed to talk about it.

'Tell me what happened,' she said.

'He was a cop, a gendarme. Claude, same name as me. He blundered into a farmhouse where my group was meeting. We had maps on the table, rifles stacked in the corner, and Bern was showing the Frenchies how to wire a time bomb.' Luke gave an odd kind of laugh, with no humour in it. 'Damn fool tried to arrest us.'

'What did you do?' Billie whispered.

'Took him outside and shot him in the back of the head.'

'Oh, my God.'

She took his hand and they walked around the long, narrow pool hand in hand. He told her another story, about a woman Resistance fighter who had been captured and tortured, and Billie cried. The afternoon cooled, and still the grim details spilled out of him: cars blown up, German officers assassinated, Jewish families led away to unknown destinations.

Finally he stumbled. 'I'm so tired,' he said. 'I've been sleeping badly.'

She hailed a taxi and took him to his hotel.

He was staying at the Carlton. She recalled that his family was wealthy. He had a corner suite. There was a grand piano in the living room and—something she had never seen before—a telephone extension in the bathroom.

She called room service and ordered chicken soup and scrambled eggs, hot rolls and cold milk. He sat on the couch and began to tell another story. Before he could finish it, the food came.

Billie signed the bill and tipped the waiter. When she turned around, Luke was asleep.

She woke him just long enough to get him into the bedroom and onto the bed. 'Don't leave,' he mumbled, then his eyes closed again.

She took off his boots and loosened his tie, then sat on the edge of the bed watching him for a while, remembering that long drive to Newport almost two years ago.

She slipped off her jacket and skirt. Then, in her underwear and stockings, she lay down on the bed. She got her arms around his shoulders, put his head on her bosom, and held him. 'Everything's all right, now,' she said. 'When you wake up, I'll still be here.'

AT DAWN, when he had been asleep for twelve hours, he got up to go to the bathroom. He got back into bed a couple of minutes later, wearing only his underwear. He put his arms around her and hugged her. 'Something I forgot to tell you, something important,' he said.

'What?'

'In France, I thought about you all the time. Every day.'

'Did you?' she whispered. 'Did you really?' But he did not answer.

He had gone back to sleep. She lay in his embrace, thinking about him in France, risking his life and remembering her; and she was so happy she felt her heart would burst.

At eight o'clock in the morning, she called in and said she was sick. It was the first day she had taken off for illness in more than a year in the military. She had a bath, got dressed and ordered coffee and cornflakes from room service.

She was reading the *Washington Post* when Luke came stumbling out of the bedroom in his underwear, his jaw blue with stubble. She smiled at him, happy that he was awake.

'How long did I sleep?

She checked her wristwatch. 'About eighteen hours.'

'I haven't slept like that for a year.' He rubbed his eyes. 'You stayed all night?'

'You asked me to.'

He went to the phone and ordered breakfast from room service.

Billie had never spent the night with a man, so she did not know what to expect in the morning, but this disappointed her. It was so unromantic. She was reminded of her brothers waking up—they, too, emerged stubbly, grouchy and ravenous.

He sat beside her on the couch. 'I talked a lot yesterday.'

'That's the truth. About five hours straight.'

He took her hands. 'I'm so glad we met again.'

Her heart jumped. 'Me, too.'

'I'd like to kiss you.'

She felt a sudden leaping sensation inside, but she held back. The war had brought about a new moral laxity in Washington, but she was not part of it. She clasped her hands in her lap and said, 'I sure don't aim to kiss you until you're dressed.'

He gave her a sceptical look. 'Are you afraid of compromising yourself? We already spent the night together.'

'I stayed here because you begged me to.'

'I appreciate it.'

'Then don't imply I've already compromised myself so that anything else I might do makes no difference.'

He gave a big sigh. 'Well, I didn't intend to imply that. You're making a hell of a fuss about a casual remark.'

'Too darn casual.'

There was a knock at the door.

She did not want a waiter to see her with an undressed man. 'Get in the bedroom.'

He went into the bedroom. Billie opened the suite door and a waitress brought in the room service cart. 'There you go, Miss,' she said.

Billie flushed. There was an insult in that 'Miss'. She signed the bill but did not tip. 'There you go,' she said, and the waitress left.

Billie heard the shower running. She felt exhausted. She had spent hours in the grip of a profound romantic passion, then in a few minutes it had turned sour. How could such things happen? Whatever the reason, he had made her feel cheap.

Well, she thought, if I don't like it, why am I still here?

She put on her hat and left the suite, closing the door quietly behind her.

SHE SAW HIM almost every day for the next four weeks.

At first he was in Q Building for daily debriefing sessions. He would seek her out at lunch time, and they would eat together in the cafeteria or take sandwiches to the park. At the end of the week he asked her for a date, and they saw the movie of *Jane Eyre*. On Sunday they went canoeing on the Potomac. There was a spirit of recklessness in Washington. The city was full of young men on their way to the front or back home on leave. They wanted to gamble, drink, dance and make love because they might never have another chance. The Allies were winning the war, but the bubble of exuberance was burst daily by news of relatives, neighbours and college friends killed and wounded on the front line.

Luke put on a little weight and the haunted look went from his eyes. A little of his boyishness came back.

They talked endlessly and had a major fight about twice a week. Each followed the pattern of their first row, in his hotel suite. He would say something high-handed, or make a decision about their evening's plans without consulting her. She would protest hotly, and he would accuse her of overreacting. She would get angry and, in the heat of the argument, would make some wild assertion she knew to be false. Then he would say there was no point in talking to her, because she was willing to say anything to win an argument. But unlike the first fight when she left, he would walk out. Within minutes, she would be distraught. She would seek him out and beg him to forget it and be friends. At first he would be stony-faced; then she would say something that made him laugh, and he would melt.

But in all that time she did not go to his hotel, and when she kissed him it was a chaste brush of the lips, always in a public place.

On Friday afternoon Luke was waiting for Billie in the lobby of Q Building when she left for the day. She could see by his face that something bad had happened. 'What's wrong?' she said immediately.

'I'm going back to France. I leave on Monday morning. Bern, too.'

Tears came to her eyes. She swallowed hard. 'Two days.'

'I've got to pack.'

'I'll help you.'

They went to his hotel. As soon as they were inside the door she pulled him to her, and tilted her face to be kissed. This time there was nothing chaste about it. Then she slipped off her coat and said, 'Touch my breasts. Please.' And his hands closed over her small breasts. She shut her eyes and concentrated on the sensation.

They broke apart, and she stared at him hungrily, memorising his face. She wanted never to forget the particular blue of his eyes, the lock of dark hair that fell over his forehead, the curve of his jaw. 'I want a photo of you,' she said.

'I might have a family photo. Let me look.' He went into the bedroom. She followed him.

His battered brown leather bag lay on a stand. He took out a silver picture frame that opened up like a book. Inside were two photographs, one on each side. He slipped a picture out and handed it to her. It showed a younger Luke in a polo shirt. With him were an older couple, plus twin boys of around fifteen, and a little girl.

'I can't take this. It's your picture of your family,' she said.

'I want you to have it. That's me, I'm part of my family.'

'Did you take it to France with you?'

'Yes.'

'There are two photos in that frame. Show me the other one.'

He seemed reluctant, but opened it. The second picture had been cut out of the Radcliffe yearbook. It was a photo of Billie.

She burst into tears. He had cut her picture out of the yearbook and carried it, alongside the photo of his family, all that time his life was in such danger.

'Why are you crying?' he said.

'Because you love me,' she replied.

'It's true,' he said. 'I've loved you since Pearl Harbor weekend.'

Her passion turned to rage. 'How can you say that? You left me.'

'If we'd become lovers then, it would have destroyed Anthony.'

'How could you put Anthony's happiness before mine. We could have had each other for two years!' The tears streamed down her cheeks. 'Now we've only got two days—two lousy days!'

'Then stop crying and kiss me again,' he said.

They made love all weekend, frantic with desire and sorrow, knowing they might never meet again.

After Luke left on Monday morning, Billie cried for two days.

Eight weeks later she discovered she was pregnant.

6.30PM: 'YES, WE DATED,' Billie said as they went down the stairs.

They came to the door of the building. 'Were we in love?' Luke asked. He looked hard at her, studying her expression.

'Oh, sure,' she said, and although her tone was light, there was a catch in her voice. 'I thought you were the only man in the world.'

How could he have let a woman like this slip away from him? It seemed a tragedy worse than losing his memory. 'But you learned better and married Bern.'

'Yes.'

'What went wrong with him?'

'Conflicting values. For Bern, politics came above all else.'

'Do you have anyone now?'

'Sure. His name's Harold Brodsky.'

Luke felt foolish. Of course she had someone. 'I guess he shares your values.'

'Yes. The most important thing in his life is his child—he's a widower—and after that comes his academic work.'

'Which is?'

'Iodine chemistry. I feel the same about my work.' She smiled. 'I may not be starry-eyed about men, but I guess I'm still idealistic about unravelling the mysteries of the human mind.'

This brought Luke back to his immediate crisis. 'I wish you could unravel the mystery of my mind.'

'It's strange,' she said. 'Maybe you suffered a cranial injury that left no visible trace. You're not an alcoholic or a drug abuser, I can tell by looking at you.'

'Which leaves . . . ?'

She shook her head. 'You certainly aren't schizophrenic. You couldn't have been given the combination of drugs and electroconvulsive therapy that could have caused—' She stopped suddenly, looking alluringly startled, mouth open, eyes wide.

'What?' Luke said.

'I just remembered Joseph Bellow. He was admitted late yesterday, after I'd gone home. Then he was discharged in the night—which was real strange.'

'What was wrong with him?'

'He was a schizophrenic.' She paled. 'Let's check his file.'

She turned and ran back up the stairs to a room marked RECORDS OFFICE. Luke followed. There was no one inside. Billie turned on the light, then opened a drawer and pulled out a folder. She read aloud: 'White male, six feet one inch tall, one hundred and eighty pounds, thirty-seven years old.'

'You think it was me,' Luke said.

She nodded. 'The patient was given a treatment that could cause global amnesia.'

'My God.' If she was right, this had been done to him deliberately. That made sense and explained why he had been followed around—presumably to make sure the treatment had worked. 'Who did this?'

'My colleague, Dr Leonard Ross, admitted the patient. A patient should normally be kept under observation for days before any treatment is given. And I can't imagine the medical justification for discharging the patient immediately afterwards. This is very irregular.'

'Sounds like Ross is in trouble.'

Billie sighed. 'If I complain, people will say I'm bitter because he got the job I wanted, Director of Research here.'

'When did that happen?'

'Today.'

Luke was startled. 'A hospital superior must have promised him the promotion in return for doing this irregular treatment.'

'No.' Billie shook her head. 'The trust that's funding the post, the Sowerby Foundation, insisted on Ross for the job.'

'But who at the foundation would want me to lose my memory?'

'I can guess who,' Billie said. 'Anthony Carroll. He's on the board.'

Luke recalled that Anthony was the CIA man mentioned by Elspeth. 'That still leaves the question why.'

'Well at least we have someone to ask,' Billie said, and she picked up the phone and dialled.

'Let me speak to Anthony Carroll,' Billie said. 'This is Dr Josephson. OK, have him call me at home one hour from now.'

'I thought this Anthony was a friend,' Luke said.

'Yeah.' Billie nodded, a worried frown on her face. 'So did I.'

7.30PM: BERN LIVED in a neighbourhood of large homes and foreign embassies. His apartment had an Iberian theme, with ornate Spanish colonial furniture, twisted shapes in dark wood. The white walls were hung with paintings of sun-baked landscapes. Luke recalled Billie saying that Bern had fought in the Spanish Civil War. It was easy to imagine him as a fighter. His dark hair was receding now, but there was a hard set to his face and a knowing look in his grey eyes.

Bern shook Luke's hand warmly and gave him strong coffee in a small cup. 'What the hell is going on, old buddy?' Bern asked.

Luke sat down and related what he and Billie had discovered at the hospital. Then he said, 'Here's what I think happened to me. I don't know if you're going to buy it, but I'm hoping you can shed some light on the mystery.'

'I'll do what I can.'

'I came to Washington on Monday, to see an army general for some mysterious purpose that I wouldn't tell anyone about. My wife was worried about me and called Anthony, who made a breakfast date with me for Tuesday morning.'

'It makes sense. Anthony's your oldest friend. You were roommates already when I met you.'

'The next bit is more speculative. At breakfast Anthony put

something in my coffee to make me fall asleep, then drove me to Georgetown Mind Hospital. He waited until Billie left for the day, checked me in under a false name, then got hold of Dr Len Ross. Using his position as a board member of the Sowerby Foundation, he persuaded Ross to give me a treatment that would destroy my memory.'

Luke waited for Bern to say the whole thing was ludicrous, but he did not. To Luke's surprise he simply said, 'But for God's sake, why?'

Luke began to feel better. If Bern believed him he might help. He said, 'For the moment, let's concentrate on how, rather than why. He checked me out of the hospital, dressed me in rags and dumped me in Union Station with a sidekick to keep an eye on me and make sure the amnesia treatment had worked.'

'But he must have known you'd find out the truth sooner or later.'

'He had to calculate that after a few days or weeks I would figure out who I was. But by then the trail would have gone cold. Billie probably would have forgotten about the mystery patient—and Ross would have destroyed his records.'

Bern nodded thoughtfully. 'A risky plan, but one with a good chance of success.'

'I'm surprised you're not more sceptical.'

Bern shrugged. 'We've all been in secret work. These things happen.'

Luke felt sure Bern was keeping something back. 'Bern, if there's something else you know, for God's sake, tell me.'

'There is something—but I don't want to get anyone into trouble.'

Luke's heart leaped in hope. 'Tell me, please. I'm desperate.'

Bern took a deep breath. 'Towards the end of the war, Billie and Anthony worked on a special project for OSS, the Truth Drug Committee. They were looking for drugs that would affect prisoners under interrogation. After the war, Billie went back to college and did her doctoral thesis on the effects of various legal drugs such as nicotine on people's mental states. When she finally became a professor, she continued to work on the same area, concentrating on how drugs and other factors affect memory.'

'But not for the CIA.'

'That's what I thought. But I was wrong. In 1950, the Agency started a project about mind control codenamed Bluebird. They financed a whole series of legitimate research projects in universities, channelling the money through trusts to conceal their true source. And they financed Billie's work.'

'How did she feel about that?'

'We fought about it. I said it was wrong; the CIA was planning to brainwash people. She said that all scientific knowledge could be used for good or evil; she was doing invaluable research and she didn't care who paid the bill.'

'Is that why you divorced?'

'Sort of. In 1952 I wrote a screenplay about a secret government agency that brainwashed unsuspecting citizens, but I didn't tell Billie. The movie came out in 1953 and was a huge hit. My career was made—I was deluged with offers from the studios.'

'And Billie?'

'I took her to the premiere. She went ape. She said I'd used confidential information I got from her. She was sure the CIA would withdraw her funding. It was the end of our marriage.'

'That's what Billie meant when she said you had a conflict of values.'

'She's right. She should have married you.'

Luke's heart missed a beat. He was curious to know why Bern said that, but he postponed the question. 'I assume the CIA didn't cut off her funding.'

'No.' Bern looked bitterly angry. 'They destroyed my career instead. I was subjected to a loyalty investigation. Of course, I had been a communist, right up until the end of the war, so I made an easy target. I was blacklisted in Hollywood.'

'What did you do?'

'I had a couple of bad years, then I thought of a series of children's books.' He pointed to a bookcase. The bright jackets made a splash of colour. 'I wrote the first story under a pseudonym. The book was a big best seller, and I've written two a year ever since.'

'Now I understand why you didn't react with total incredulity to my story,' Luke said.

'Yes,' Bern said. 'I believe Anthony did this. But I don't have the least idea why.'

8.00PM: BILLIE SAT at her dressing table, freshening her make-up. She could hear television gunfire downstairs: Larry and Becky-Ma were watching *Wagon Train*.

She did not feel like a date with Harold Brodsky tonight. She was angry about not getting the job she wanted, bewildered by what Anthony had done, and confused and threatened to find that the old chemistry between herself and Luke was as powerful as ever.

The phone rang. She jumped up and crossed the room to the extension by the bed, but Larry had already picked up in the hallway. She heard Anthony say, 'This is the CIA. Washington is about to be invaded by an army of bouncing cabbages.'

Larry giggled. 'Uncle Anthony, it's you!'

'If you are approached by a cabbage do not, repeat, do not attempt to reason with it.'

'You're making this up!' Larry laughed.

Billie said, 'Anthony, I'm on the extension.'

Anthony said, 'Get your jammies on, Larry, OK?'

'OK,' said Larry. He hung up.

'Anthony, what the hell are you up to?' Billie asked. 'I could tell you were lying last time we spoke, but I didn't know what the truth was then. Now I do. I know what you did to Luke at my hospital last night. I want an explanation.'

'I can't really talk about this on the phone. If we could meet sometime in the next few days—'

'I want your story right now.'

'I'll explain everything if you'll meet me tomorrow.'

She almost agreed, then she remembered what he had done. 'You went behind my back, right in my own hospital. Tell me the truth right now or I'll go to the FBI the minute I hang up.'

It was dangerous to threaten men—it often made them obstinate. But she knew how the CIA hated and feared interference from the FBI, especially when the Agency was working on the borderline of legality, which was most of the time.

He sighed. 'You may find this hard to believe.'

'Try me.'

'Well, here goes. Luke is a spy, Billie.'

'Don't be absurd.'

'He's an agent for Moscow. He's been passing rocket secrets to the Soviets for years. How do you think they managed to put their Sputnik into orbit while our satellite was still on the laboratory bench? They had the benefit of all our research as well as their own.'

'Anthony, we've both known Luke for twenty years. He'd never betray his country.'

'People do. Remember, when he was with the French Resistance he was working with the communists. They were on our side then, but obviously he continued after the war.'

Billie sat down, feeling stunned. 'Do you have evidence?'

'I have *proof*—top secret blueprints he gave a known KGB officer.'

'But even if all this is true, why did you wipe out his memory?'

'To save his life. The CIA was going to kill him.'

'Why not just put him on trial as a spy?'

'And have the whole world know that our security is so lousy the Soviets have been getting all our rocket secrets for years?'

'So what happened?'

'I persuaded them to try this. Nobody knows except the Director of the CIA and the President. And it would have worked, if only he'd believed that he lost his memory after a night of drinking and lived the life of a bum for a while. I could have kept the lid on. Even he would never have known what secrets he gave away. Is he with you now?'

'No.' Billie felt the hairs prickle on the back of her neck.'

'I need to talk to him before he does himself any more damage.'

Acting on instinct, Billie lied. 'I don't know where he is.'

'You wouldn't hide anything from me, would you?'

'You've already said your organisation wanted to kill Luke. It would be dumb of me to tell you where he is, if I knew. But I don't.'

'Billie, listen to me. I'm his only hope. Tell him to call me, if you want to save his life.'

'I'll think about it,' Billie said, but Anthony had already hung up.

8.30PM: LUKE PUT DOWN the phone with a shaky hand. Bern said, 'What did Billie say? You look like a ghost!'

'Anthony says I'm a Soviet agent,' Luke told him. 'The CIA was going to kill me, but Anthony persuaded them that it would be just as effective to wipe my memory. Could it be true?'

'Hell, no.'

'You can't be sure of that.'

'Yes, I can. Because I *was* a Soviet agent and you ended my career.'

'How?'

Bern stood up. 'I'm going to make you a sandwich.'

Luke realised he was painfully hungry. 'That sounds great.'

They went into the kitchen. Bern opened the refrigerator and took out a loaf of rye bread, butter, corned beef and an onion.

'It was in the war,' Bern said, as he buttered four slices of bread. 'The French Resistance was divided into Gaullists and communists, and they were manoeuvring for position. Roosevelt and Churchill wanted to make sure the communists couldn't win an election. So the Gaullists were getting all the guns and ammunition.'

'How did I feel about that?'

Bern layered corned beef and onion rings on the bread. 'You just wanted to beat the Nazis and go home, but I had another agenda. I wanted to even things up.'

'How?'

'I tipped off the communists about a parachute drop we were expecting, so they could ambush us and steal our ordnance.' He shook his head ruefully. 'They screwed up royally. They attacked us as soon as the stuff hit the ground. So you knew we had been betrayed. And I was the obvious suspect.'

'What did I do?'

'You offered me a deal. I had to stop working for Moscow, right then, and you would keep quiet about what I had done, for ever. We both kept our promises, but our friendship was never the same.'

'If I'd been a communist, I would have covered up for you.'

'Absolutely.'

'So Anthony is mistaken.'

'Or lying.' Bern put the sandwiches on plates. 'Soda?'

'Sure.'

Bern took two bottles of Coke from the refrigerator and opened them. He handed Luke a plate and a bottle, picked up his own, and led the way back into the living room.

Luke finished the sandwich in a few bites.

Bern said, 'If Anthony is lying, what was his real reason for making you lose your memory?'

'It has to be connected with my sudden departure from Cape Canaveral. I must have learned something so important that I had to rush to the Pentagon to talk to them about it. I guess I told Anthony what I had found out and he thought it was so important that he had to wipe my memory of it.'

'I wonder what the hell it was.'

'I guess my first step to finding out is to go to my hotel room and look through my stuff. Maybe I'll find a clue.'

'If Anthony wiped your memory, he must have gone through your possessions too.'

'But there may be something he didn't recognise as relevant.'

'And then?'

'The only other place to look would be Cape Canaveral. I'll fly back tonight or tomorrow morning.'

'Spend the night here,' Bern said. 'My instincts tell me you're in danger. I don't like the idea of you spending the night alone. Go to the Carlton, pick up your stuff, and come back here. I'll take you to the airport in the morning.'

Luke said, 'You've been a heck of a good friend to me over this.'

Bern shrugged. 'We go back a long way.'

'But you just told me that, after that incident in France, our friendship was never the same.'

'That's true.' Bern gave Luke a candid look. 'Your attitude was that a man who betrayed you once would betray you twice.'

'I can believe that,' Luke said thoughtfully. 'I was wrong, though, wasn't I?'

'Yes,' Bern said. 'You were.'

9.30PM: ANTHONY'S YELLOW CADILLAC was parked outside the Carlton Hotel. Pete hurried out of the building and came to the car. 'Ackie called in. Luke is at Bernard Rothsten's place.'

'At last,' Anthony said. He had posted agents outside Bern's building and Billie's house.

Pete added, 'When he leaves, Ackie will follow him on the motorcycle. Do you think he'll come here?'

'He may. I'll wait.' There were two more agents in the hotel lobby who would alert Anthony if Luke should go in by another entrance.

A little later a taxicab pulled into the hotel's driveway, and Luke got out. He was wearing a navy topcoat and a grey hat. Across the street, Ackie Horwitz pulled up on his motorcycle. Anthony got out of his car and strolled towards the hotel entrance.

Luke paid the taxi driver. He glanced at Anthony but did not recognise him.

LUKE KNEW he had been followed from Bern's apartment by a man on a motorcycle. Now he was strung taut, all his senses on alert.

The lobby of the Carlton looked like a grand drawing room, full of reproduction French furniture. It was a luxurious place, designed to soothe the nerves of jangled travellers. It did nothing for Luke.

Scanning the room, he quickly identified two men who had the air of agents: one sitting on a sofa, the other near the elevator. They were dressed in business suits. They definitely were not out for an evening in expensive restaurants and bars. He thought of walking right out again—but where would that leave him? He approached the reception desk, gave his name, and asked for the key to his room. As he turned away, a stranger spoke to him. 'Hey, Luke!'

It was the man who had walked into the hotel behind him.

Luke said, 'I'm afraid I don't know who you are.'

'Anthony Carroll. I'm so glad I've caught up with you at last!' He held out his hand to shake.

Luke tensed. He still didn't know whether Anthony was enemy or friend. He shook hands and said, 'I have a lot of questions to ask you.'

'And I'm ready to answer them.'

Luke paused, wondering where to begin. Anthony did not look like a man who would betray an old friend. He had an open face. In the end, Luke said, 'How could you do this to me? I'm not a spy.'

'It's not that simple. I had to do it—I was trying to save your life.'

'Neither Bern nor Billie believes your story about my working for Moscow.'

'They don't know everything.'

'What do you know that they don't?'

'I'll tell you. But we can't talk here. Shall we go to my office? It's five minutes away.'

'Let's go to my suite,' Luke said.

Anthony hesitated, then said, 'Sure.'

They crossed the lobby. Luke checked the number on his room key: 530. 'Fifth floor,' he said to the elevator operator.

They did not speak as they went up. Luke looked at Anthony's clothes: the old camel-hair coat, the rumpled suit, the nondescript tie. Suddenly, Luke saw that the soft material of the coat sagged slightly on the right side. There was a heavy object in the pocket.

He felt cold with fear. He had not thought that Anthony would have a gun. Trying to keep his face immobile, Luke thought furiously. Could Anthony shoot him right here in the hotel?

As the elevator stopped at the fifth floor, Anthony unbuttoned his coat. For a fast draw, Luke thought. They stepped out. Luke did not know which way to go, but Anthony confidently turned right. He must have been to Luke's room already.

Luke tried to make himself calm. Anthony had the gun, but Luke had guessed Anthony's intentions. It was about even.

They reached the door and Luke took out his key. If he went inside, he was dead.

He unlocked the door and pushed it open. 'Come in,' he said. He stood aside to let his guest enter first.

Anthony hesitated, then walked past Luke through the doorway.

Luke hooked his foot around Anthony's right ankle, put both hands flat on Anthony's shoulder blades, and pushed hard. Anthony went flying. He crashed into a small table, knocking over a vase. In desperation he grabbed at a brass floor lamp, but it fell with him.

Luke pulled the door shut and ran for his life. He hurtled along the corridor, burst through the fire exit to the staircase and ran down. On the next floor, he crashed into a maid carrying a stack of towels. 'I'm sorry,' he called as towels flew everywhere.

ANTHONY KNEW, before he did it, that it was a mistake to enter the room first, but Luke left him no choice. After a stunned moment, he picked himself up and opened the door. Looking out, he saw Luke haring along the corridor. As Anthony gave chase, Luke disappeared into the stairwell.

Anthony followed, running as fast as he could. On the next floor down, he was momentarily delayed by a maid who was kneeling on the floor, picking up scattered towels. He slowed his pace to manoeuvre around her. As he did so, he heard the elevator arrive.

A couple in evening clothes emerged. Anthony barged past them into the elevator and said, 'Ground floor, and quick about it.'

The man slammed the doors and threw the lever. The elevator descended slowly.

LUKE EMERGED into the lobby next to the elevator doors. His heart sank. The two agents he had spotted earlier were standing in front of the main entrance, blocking his way out. A moment later, the elevator door opened and Anthony stepped out. Luke turned and ran back into the depths of the hotel. Behind him he heard the pounding footsteps of Anthony giving chase. There had to be a back entrance—supplies could not possibly be delivered through the main lobby.

He pushed through a curtain and found himself in a little courtyard decorated like a Mediterranean outdoor café. Barging between the tables, he made it to an exit door, emerging into a kind of butler's pantry. Half a dozen uniformed waiters were heating food in chafing dishes and arranging plates on trays. In the middle of the room was a staircase leading down. Luke pushed through the waiters and took the stairs, ignoring a voice that called, 'Excuse me, sir. You can't go down there!' As Anthony charged after him, the same voice said indignantly, 'What is this, Union Station?'

In the basement was the kitchen, a sweaty purgatory where dozens of chefs cooked for hundreds of people. They were too busy to pay attention to Luke as he dodged between the refrigerators and the ranges. At the back of the kitchen, he found a staircase going up. He guessed it led to the delivery entrance. He raced up the stairs. At the top, he burst through a door into the cold night air.

He was in a dark yard. Fifty yards to his right was a high wire fence with a closed gate. He ran towards it. He heard the door behind him bang open, and guessed that Anthony had come out.

Luke reached the gate. It was closed and secured with a big steel padlock. Heart pounding, he scrambled up the fence. As he reached the top, he heard the discreet cough of a silenced pistol. But he felt nothing. It was a hard shot, a moving target fifty yards away in the dark. He flung himself over the top. The pistol coughed again. He staggered and fell to the ground. He heard a third muffled shot. He sprang to his feet and ran, heading east. At the corner, he looked back. Anthony was nowhere in sight.

He had escaped.

10.30PM: MRS RILEY'S TUNA BAKE was as tasty as promised. For dessert, Harold served cherry pie and ice cream. Billie felt guilty. He was trying so hard to please her, but her mind was on Luke and Anthony, their shared past and their puzzling new entanglement.

After dinner Harold suggested they move to the living room. He produced a bottle of expensive French brandy and poured generous measures into two snifters. Was he trying to stiffen his own courage, Billie wondered, or lower her resistance?

Harold Brodsky was normally an entertaining talker, witty and clever, and she generally laughed a lot when she was with him, but tonight he seemed preoccupied.

He poured himself another brandy. 'I've been thinking about our future,' he said.

Billie's heart sank. He was going to propose. Yesterday she would have accepted him, but today she could hardly think about it.

He took her hand. 'I love you,' he said. 'We get on well, we have the same interests, and we both have a child. But that's not why I want to marry you. I just adore you, for no reason other than you're you. I want us to be together for ever.' He looked at her, then said, 'How do you feel?'

Billie sighed. 'I'm fond of you. Yesterday, I would have said yes, let's get married. But today I met someone from my past, and I remembered what it was like to be in love at the age of twenty-one. I don't feel that way about you, Harold.'

He was not totally discouraged. 'Who does, at our age?'

'Maybe you're right,' she said.

The doorbell rang and Billie's heart leaped.

'Who the heck is that?' Harold said angrily. He got up and went out to the hall.

Billie heard Luke's voice at the door. 'I need to talk to Billie.'

She wondered why she was so inordinately pleased.

Harold said, 'I'm not sure she wants to be disturbed right now.'

'It's important.'

'How did you know she was here?'

'Her mother told me. I'm sorry, I don't have time to dick around.' Billie heard a cry of protest from Harold, and she guessed Luke had forced his way into the house. She went into the hallway. Luke looked very shaken. 'What's happened now?' she said.

'Anthony shot at me.'

Billie was shocked. 'Anthony? My God, what got into him?'

Harold looked scared. 'What's this about a shooting?'

Luke ignored him and said to Billie, 'I'm going to the Pentagon, but I may not be believed. Will you come and back me up?'

'Sure,' she said. She took her coat off the hall stand.

Harold said, 'Billie! We were having a very important conversation.'

Luke said, 'I really need you.'

Billie hesitated. It was hard on Harold. He had obviously been planning this moment for some time. But Luke's life was in danger. 'I'm sorry,' she said to Harold. 'I have to go.' She lifted her face to be kissed, but he turned away.

'Get out of my house, both of you,' Harold said furiously.

11.00PM: ANTHONY FOUND some stationery in the desk drawer of the hotel room Pete had rented. He took out an envelope. From his pocket he took three slugs and three cartridge cases, the rounds he had fired at Luke. He put them into the envelope and sealed it, then stuffed it into his pocket. He would dispose of it later. He was doing damage control. He had very little time, but he had to be meticulous. He needed to wipe out all trace of this incident.

The assistant manager on duty came into the room. He was a small, bald man. 'Sit down, please, Mr Suchard.' Anthony showed the man his CIA identification.

'What can I do for you, Mr Carroll?' Suchard asked.

'First, I want to apologise for the little fracas we had earlier.'

Suchard nodded primly. 'Fortunately, very few guests noticed anything.'

'I'm glad we didn't disrupt your fine hotel too much, even over a matter of national security. Of course, I can't give you the details, but I hope I can rely on your discretion.'

'Indeed, you can.'

Anthony took out a roll of bills. 'The State Department has a small fund for compensation in these instances.' He slowly counted five twenties and handed them over.

'Thank you, sir,' said Suchard. 'I'm sure we can handle things.'

'If anyone questions you, it might be best to say you saw nothing.'

'Of course.' Suchard stood up. 'If there's anything else . . .'

'I'll be in touch.' Anthony nodded dismissively, and Suchard left.

Pete came in. 'The head of security at Cape Canaveral is Colonel Bill Hide.' He handed Anthony a slip of paper with the number.

Anthony dialled it and got through. 'This Anthony Carroll, CIA.'

Hide spoke with a slow, unmilitary drawl. 'Well, what can I do for you, Mr Carroll?'

'I'm calling about Dr Lucas.'

'Oh, yes?'

He sounded faintly hostile, and Anthony decided to butter him up. 'I would appreciate your advice, if you could spare a moment, Colonel.'

Hide warmed up. 'Of course, anything I can do.'

'I think you know that Dr Lucas has been behaving strangely. What would you say is his mental state?'

'He seemed normal last time I saw him, but I talked to him a few hours ago and he told me he'd lost his memory.'

'There's more to it than that. He stole a car and broke into a house, got into a fight with a cop, stuff like that.'

'My God, he's in worse shape than I thought.'

Hide was buying the story, Anthony thought with relief. He pressed on. 'We think he's not rational, but you know him better than we do. What would you say is going on?'

'Hell, I think he's suffering some kind of breakdown.' This was exactly what Anthony wanted Hide to believe. Hide continued,

'Normally, Luke is as sane as you or me. Obviously something has destabilised him.'

'He seems to think there's some kind of conspiracy against him—but you're saying we shouldn't necessarily credit that.'

'Not for a minute.'

'So we should soft-pedal this stuff. I mean, we shouldn't alert the Pentagon.'

'God, no,' Hide said worriedly. 'In fact, I'd better call them and warn them that Luke seems to have lost his marbles.'

'As you wish. Thank you, Colonel. You've set my mind at rest.'

'You're welcome.'

Anthony hung up and reviewed the situation. There was no evidence left at the hotel. He had prejudiced the Pentagon against any report Luke might make. That just left Billie's hospital.

He stood up. 'I'll be back in an hour,' he said to Pete. 'Take Malone and Curtis and bribe a room service waiter to let you into Luke's suite. I have a feeling he'll come back.'

12 MIDNIGHT: BILLIE drove the red Thunderbird into the parking lot of the Georgetown Mind Hospital and killed the engine. Colonel Lopez from the Pentagon pulled alongside her in a Ford Fairlane.

'He doesn't believe a word I say,' Luke said angrily.

'You can't blame him,' Billie reasoned. 'The assistant manager of the Carlton says no one was chased through the kitchens, and there are no cartridge cases at the loading dock.'

'Anthony cleaned up the evidence.'

'I know that, but Colonel Lopez doesn't.'

They got out of their cars and walked into the building. Billie led the two men up the stairs and along the corridor to the records office.

'I'm going to show you the file of a man named Joseph Bellow, whose physical characteristics match Luke's,' she told the colonel. 'You'll see that he was admitted on Tuesday, treated, then discharged at four o'clock on Wednesday morning. It's very unusual for a schizophrenic patient to be given treatment without observation first and it's unheard of for a patient to be released from a mental hospital at four o'clock in the morning.'

Billie opened the drawer, pulled out the Bellow file and opened it.

It was empty. 'Oh, my God,' she said.

Luke stared at the folder in disbelief. 'I saw the papers myself less than six hours ago!'

Lopez stood up with a weary air. 'Well, I guess that's it.'

Luke had the nightmare feeling that he was living in a surreal world in which people could do what they liked to him, and he could never prove it had happened.

'Wait,' Billie said. 'The register will show his admission. It's kept at the reception desk.'

They went down to the lobby. Billie said. 'Let me see the register, please, Charlie.'

'Right away, Dr Josephson.' The young black man behind the counter searched around for a moment. 'Where did that thing go?' he said. 'I know it was here a couple of hours ago.'

Billie's face was like thunder. 'Tell me something. Has Dr Ross been here tonight?'

'Yes, ma'am. He left a few minutes ago.'

'Next time you see him, ask him where the register went.'

Luke turned to Lopez. 'Before we saw you tonight, Colonel, had someone else talked to you about me?'

Lopez hesitated. 'Yes,' he admitted. 'I guess you're entitled to know. We got a call from a Colonel Hide down in Cape Canaveral. He said the CIA had reported that you were behaving irrationally.'

Luke nodded grimly. 'Anthony again.'

Billie said to Lopez, 'I don't blame you for not believing us, when we have no evidence.'

'I didn't say I don't believe you,' Lopez said.

Luke was startled, and looked at the colonel with new hope.

Lopez went on, 'I could believe you imagined that a CIA man chased you around the Carlton. I might even accept that you and the doctor conspired to pretend there used to be a file and it disappeared. But I don't believe that Charlie here is in on the conspiracy. There must be a daily register, and it's gone. I don't think you took it, but who did? Someone has something to hide.'

'So you believe me?' Luke said.

'Something is going on. And it must have to do with that rocket launch. I'm going to order a full security alert at Cape Canaveral.'

'But what about Anthony?'

'I have a friend at the CIA. I'm going to tell him your story, and say I don't know whether it's true or not, but I'm concerned.'

'That's not going to get us far!' Luke protested. 'We need to know what's going on, why they wiped my memory!'

'I agree,' Lopez said. 'But I can't do any more. The rest is up to you.'

'So, I'm on my own,' Luke said.

'No, you're not,' said Billie. 'You're not on your own.'

Part Four

1.00am: Billie parked her car around the corner from the entrance of the Carlton. 'I'll go first,' she said. 'If there's anyone suspicious in the lobby, I'll come right out again. When you see me take my coat off, you'll know it's all clear.'

Luke was not comfortable with this plan. 'What if Anthony's there?'

'He won't shoot me.'

She got out of the car and they approached the hotel separately. Luke watched Billie go in, enjoying her jaunty walk. He could see through the glass doors into the lobby. A porter approached her and Luke guessed she was saying, 'I'm Mrs Lucas, my husband will be along in a moment.' Then she took off her coat.

Luke entered the hotel. For the porter's benefit he said, 'I want to make a call before we go upstairs, honey.' Next to the reception desk was a phone booth with a seat. Luke went inside. Billie followed him and closed the door. He put a dime in the slot and called the hotel. He angled the handset so that Billie could hear.

'Sheraton-Carlton, good morning.'

'Room five-thirty, please.'

'Sir, it's past one o'clock—is this an emergency?'

'Dr Lucas asked me to call no matter how late.'

'Very good.'

There was a pause, then a ringing tone. After four rings, the phone was picked up. So Anthony, or one of his men, was lying in wait.

A voice said, 'Hello?' It was not Anthony.

Luke said tipsily, 'Hey, Ronnie, this is Tim. We're waitin' for ya.'

The man grunted with irritation. 'Drunk,' he muttered, as if speaking to someone else. 'You got the wrong room, buddy.' He hung up.

'Someone there?' Billie said.

'Maybe more than one.'

'I know how to get them out. I did it in Lisbon, during the war.'

They left the phone booth. Luke noticed Billie discreetly pick up a book of matches from an ashtray by the elevator. On the fifth floor they found room 530 and went past it. Billie opened a door to reveal a linen closet. 'Perfect,' she said. 'Is there a fire alarm near by?'

Luke looked around and saw an alarm of the type that could be set off by breaking a pane of glass with the little hammer hanging next to it. 'Right there,' he said.

'Good.' In the closet, sheets and blankets stood in neat stacks on slatted wooden shelves. Billie unfolded a blanket and dropped it on the floor. She did the same with several more until she had a pile. She took a breakfast order from a doorknob and lit it with a match. As it flared up, she put the flame to the blankets. 'This is why you should never smoke in bed,' she said.

As the flames blazed up, Billie piled on additional bed linen. Soon smoke began to fill the corridor. 'Time to sound the alarm,' she said. 'We don't want anyone to get hurt.'

Luke broke the fire alarm glass and pressed the large red button inside. A moment later, a loud ringing shattered the silence.

He and Billie retreated along the corridor until they could only just see the door of Luke's suite through the smoke. The corridor filled with people coughing and fumbling through the smoke towards the stairwell.

The door to room 530 opened slowly. Luke saw a tall man step into the corridor: Pete. He drew back to avoid being recognised. The figure hesitated, then joined the rush for the stairs. Two more men came out and followed him.

'All clear,' Luke said, and he and Billie entered the suite.

'Oh, my God,' said Billie. 'It's the same room. I can't believe it.'

He stood still, watching. 'What happened here?' he asked.

She shook her head wonderingly. 'It's hard to imagine that you don't remember.' She walked around. 'There was a grand piano in that corner,' she said. She looked into the bathroom. 'And a phone in here. I had never seen a phone in a bathroom.'

Luke waited.

'You stayed here in the war,' she said at last. 'We made love here.'

He looked into the bedroom. 'On that bed, I guess.'

'Not just on the bed.' She giggled. 'How young we were.'

The thought of making love to this woman was unbearably exciting. 'My God, I wish I could remember,' he said, and his voice sounded thick with desire.

To his surprise, she blushed.

He turned aside and picked up the phone. He dialled the operator. He wanted to make sure the fire did not spread. 'This is Mr Davies. I sounded the alarm,' he said rapidly. 'The fire is in a linen closet near room five-forty.' He hung up.

Billie was looking around, her emotional moment over. 'Your clothes are here,' she said.

Lying on the bed were a grey tweed sports jacket and a pair of charcoal pants. On the floor was a pair of wing-tip shoes. Luke opened the drawer of the bedside table and found a wallet, a chequebook and a slim appointments diary with a list of phone numbers in the back. He looked quickly through its pages and found the current week, but there were no obvious clues.

A well-worn black leather suitcase rested open on a stand. Luke rummaged through it, finding clean shirts and underwear, a notebook half full of mathematical calculations, and a paperback book.

Billie looked in the bathroom. 'Shaving gear, toiletry bag, toothbrush, that's all.'

Luke opened all the cupboards and drawers in the bedroom, and Billie did the same in the living room. He found a black wool topcoat and a black Homburg hat in a closet, but nothing else.

'Your phone messages are here on the desk,' Billie said. 'From Bern, from a Colonel Hide, and from someone called Marigold.'

'She's my secretary in Huntsville. Colonel Hide said she had made my flight reservations.'

'I wonder if you told her the purpose of the trip.'

'It's possible.' He looked at the phone numbers in the back of the diary. 'Bingo,' he said. 'Marigold—Home.' He sat at the desk and dialled the number.

The phone was answered by a sleepy woman with a slow Alabama accent.

He said, 'I'm sorry to call so late. Is this Marigold?'

'Dr Lucas! Thank God you've called. What in heaven happened to you? No one knew where you were at—and now I hear tell you lost your memory. Is that so?'

'Yes, but I'm hoping you might help me figure things out.'

'If I can . . .'

'Did I tell you why I suddenly decided to go to Washington on Monday?'

'You sure didn't. You just said you needed to fly to Washington via Huntsville, that you wanted to stop over here for a couple of hours.'

'I wonder why.'

'Then you said something kind of strange. You asked me not to tell anyone that you were coming here.'

'Ah. So it was a secret visit?'

'Yes. And I've kept it secret.'

The fire alarm stopped ringing and Luke realised he had run out of time. 'I have to go now,' he told Marigold. 'Thanks for your help.' He hung up.

'I've packed your stuff,' Billie said.

'Thanks,' he said. He took his own black coat and hat from the closet and put them on. 'Now let's get out of here before the spooks come back.'

THEY DROVE to an all-night diner and ordered coffee. 'I wonder when the first flight to Huntsville leaves in the morning,' Luke said.

'We need the Official Airline Guide,' Billie said. 'I bet Bern has one. It's the kind of thing writers like. They're always looking stuff up.'

'He's probably asleep.'

Billie stood up. 'Then I'll wake him.'

She went to the payphone beside the rest rooms. Luke sipped his coffee, watching her. She looked bewitching, and he ached with desire for her.

She returned and said, 'He's going to join us and bring the book.'

Luke checked his watch. It was 2.00am. 'I'll probably go straight to the airport from here. I hope there's an early flight.'

Billie frowned. 'Is there a deadline?'

'There might be. I keep asking myself: what could have made me drop everything and rush to Washington? It has to be something to do with the rocket—a threat to the launch.'

'Sabotage?'

'Yes. And if I'm right, I have to prove it before ten thirty tonight.'

'Do you want me to fly to Huntsville with you?'

'You have to take care of Larry.'

'I can leave him with Bern.'

Luke shook his head. 'I don't think so . . . thanks.'

'You always were an independent son of a gun.'

'It's not that,' he said. He wanted her to understand. 'I'd love you to come with me. That's the trouble—I'd like it too much. Did I always like you so much, or is this new?'

'This is not new. We fight like hell. But we adore one another.'

'You said we were lovers, once. Was it good?'

She looked at him with tears in her eyes. 'The best.'

'Then how come I'm not married to you?'

She began to cry. 'Because . . .' She wiped her face and blurted out, 'You got so mad at me, you didn't speak to me for five years.'

1945: ANTHONY'S PARENTS had a farm near Charlottesville, Virginia. It was a big white timber-framed house with rambling wings that contained a dozen bedrooms.

Luke arrived there on the Friday after Japan surrendered. Anthony's mother showed him to a bedroom where he changed out of his uniform—he now held the rank of major—and put on a black cashmere sports jacket. As he was tying his tie, Anthony looked in. 'Cocktails in the drawing room whenever you're ready,' he said.

'I'll be right there,' Luke said. 'Which room is Billie in?'

'The girls are in the other wing, I'm afraid,' Anthony said. 'The

Admiral is old-fashioned about that sort of thing.' His father had spent his life in the navy.

'No problem,' Luke said with a shrug. He had spent the last three years moving around occupied Europe at night: he would be able to find Billie's room in the dark.

When he went downstairs he found all his old friends waiting. As well as Anthony and Billie, there were Elspeth, Bern and Bern's girlfriend Peg. Luke had spent much of the war with Bern and Anthony, and every leave with Billie, but he had not seen Elspeth or Peg since 1941. The Admiral handed him a martini and he took a satisfying gulp. This was a time to celebrate if ever there was one.

Luke studied them over dinner, comparing them with the golden youths who been so worried, four years ago, about being expelled from Harvard. Elspeth was painfully thin after three years on rations in wartime London. Peg, who had been a dowdy girl with a big heart, was now smartly dressed, but her skilfully made-up face looked hardened and cynical. Bern at twenty-seven looked ten years older. This had been his second war and he had been wounded three times. Anthony had seen some action, but had spent most of the war in Washington. Billie had spent two years undercover in Lisbon, and had killed a man there, but she was still a bundle of radiant energy, gay at one moment and fierce at the next.

'We should drink a toast,' Luke said, lifting his wineglass. 'To those who survived—and those who did not.'

They all drank, then Bern said, 'I have another. To the men who broke the back of the Nazi war machine—the Red Army.'

They all drank again, but the Admiral looked displeased.

Coffee was served in the drawing room. Luke handed the cups around. As he offered cream and sugar to Billie, she said in a low voice, 'East wing, last door on the left.'

At ten thirty the Admiral insisted the men move to the billiard room. He poured himself a tumbler of bourbon and took Luke to the locked display rack at the far end of the room to show him his guns.

'I know and respect your family, Luke,' the Admiral said as they examined an Enfield rifle. 'Your father is a very great man.'

'Thank you,' Luke said. His father had spent the war helping to run the Office of Price Administration.

'You'll have to think of your family when you choose a wife, my boy. Whoever becomes Mrs Lucas will have a place waiting for her in the upper reaches of American society. You must pick a girl who can carry that off.'

'I'll bear that in mind, Admiral,' Luke said, putting the rifle back.

The Admiral put a hand on his arm, 'Whatever you do, don't get stuck with that little Jewess—she's not worthy of you.'

Luke gritted his teeth. 'If you'll excuse me, this is something I'd rather discuss with my own father.'

'But your father doesn't know about her, does he?'

Luke flushed. The Admiral had scored a point. Luke and Billie had not met one another's parents. He said, 'Forgive me if I warn you that these remarks are personally offensive to me.'

The room went quiet, but Luke's veiled threat passed over the head of the drunken Admiral. 'I understand that, son, but I may know more about the lady in question than you do.'

'The hell you do,' Luke said.

The Admiral put his arm round Luke's shoulders. 'Look, son, I'm a man, I understand. There's no harm in pronging a little tart, we've all—'

He never finished the sentence. Luke shoved him away. The Admiral staggered back, arms flailing, and his glass of bourbon went flying through the air. He sat down hard on the rug.

Anthony, white-faced, grabbed Luke's arm. 'Luke, for God's sake, what do you think you're doing?'

Bern stepped between them and the fallen Admiral. 'Calm down, both of you,' he said.

'The hell with *calm*,' Luke said. 'What kind of man invites you to his house then insults your girlfriend?'

'She is a tart,' the Admiral said. 'I should know, damn it. I paid for her abortion!'

Luke was stunned. 'Abortion?'

'Yes.' The Admiral struggled to his feet. 'Anthony got her pregnant, and I paid a thousand dollars for her to get rid of the little bastard.' His mouth twisted in a spiteful grin of triumph.

Luke looked at Anthony, but Anthony shook his head. 'I told my father it was my baby, so that he'd give me the money, but it was your child, Luke.'

Luke blushed to the roots of his hair. The drunken old Admiral had made a complete fool of him. He was the ignorant one. He thought he knew Billie, yet she had kept this a secret from him. He had fathered a child, and his girlfriend had had an abortion, and they knew about it but he did not. He was utterly humiliated.

He stormed out of the room, ran up the stairs and along the east wing. He found Billie's room and went in without knocking.

She was lying naked on the bed, reading. For a moment, the sight of her took his breath away. She looked up at him with a happy smile, then her face darkened at his expression.

'The Admiral says he paid for you to have an abortion. Is it true? Answer me!'

She nodded, began to cry and buried her face in her hands.

'So you did deceive me?'

'I'm sorry,' she sobbed. 'I wanted to have your baby with all my heart, but you were in France, and I didn't know if you were ever coming back. I had to decide all on my own.' She raised her voice. 'It was the worst time of my life.'

'You should have told me.'

Her mood changed. She sighed. 'Yes, I know. But Anthony thought I shouldn't tell anyone, and it's not difficult to persuade a girl to keep something like that a secret.'

Luke was maddened by the calm way she talked about her treachery. 'I can't live with this,' he said.

'What do you mean?'

'After you've deceived me over something so important how can I ever trust you again?'

She looked anguished. 'You're going to tell me it's over, aren't you?'

'Yes.'

She began to cry afresh. 'You idiot! You don't know anything, do you, despite the war.'

'The war taught me that nothing counts as much as loyalty.'

'You still haven't learned that when humans are under pressure, we're all willing to lie.'

'Even to people we love?'

'We lie *more* to our loved ones, because we care what they think.'

He despised such easy excuses. 'That's not my philosophy of life.'

'Lucky you,' she said bitterly. 'You come from a happy home, you've never known bereavement or rejection. You had a hard war, but you weren't crippled or tortured. Nothing bad has ever happened to you. Sure, you don't tell lies.'

'If that's how you think of me, you must be glad our relationship is over.'

'No, I'm not glad.' Tears ran down her face. 'I love you. I'm sorry I deceived you, but I'm not going to prostrate myself with guilt because I did a bad thing in a moment of crisis.'

Somewhere in the back of his mind, a small voice told him he was throwing away the most precious thing he had ever had. But he was too angry, too humiliated, and too painfully wounded to listen. He went to the door.

'Don't leave,' she pleaded.

'Go to hell,' he said, and he went out.

2.30AM: 'I CAN'T BELIEVE I gave you up,' Luke said. 'Didn't I understand what you'd been through?'

'It wasn't all your fault,' Billie said wearily. 'I thought it was, at the time, but now I can see my own role in the whole mess.'

'And so you married Bern.'

She laughed. 'I didn't marry Bern because you left me. I married him because he's one of the best men in the world. It took me years to get over you but, when I did, I fell in love with Bern.'

'And you and I became friends again?'

'Slowly. I wrote to you when Larry was born, and you came to see me. Then Anthony had a thirtieth birthday party and you showed up. You were back at Harvard, getting your doctorate, and the rest of us were in Washington—Anthony and Elspeth working for the CIA, me doing research at George Washington University, and Bern writing scripts for National Public Radio.'

'When did I marry Elspeth?'

'Nineteen fifty-four—the year I divorced Bern.'

'Do you know why I married her?'

She hesitated. 'I'm the wrong person to answer that question.'

A white Lincoln Continental pulled up outside and Bern jumped out and came into the diner.

'I'm sorry we woke you,' said Luke.

'Forget it,' Bern said. 'Here.' He tossed a thick booklet onto the table. The cover said: OFFICIAL AIRLINE GUIDE. Luke picked it up.

Billie said, 'Look for Capital Airlines—they fly to the south.'

Luke found it. 'There's a plane that leaves at six fifty-five, but it stops at every small town in Dixie, and gets to Huntsville at two twenty-three this afternoon, local time.'

Bern read over his shoulder. 'The next plane doesn't leave until nine o'clock, but it has fewer stops, so it gets you to Huntsville a few minutes before noon.'

'I'd get the later plane, but I don't relish hanging around Washington any longer than I have to,' Luke said. 'Maybe I could leave here by car, and pick up a plane somewhere down the line. The early flight's first stop is a place called Newport News. Where's that?'

'Near Norfolk, Virginia,' Billie said.

'It lands there at two minutes past eight. Can I get there in time?'

'It's two hundred miles,' Billie said. 'You can make it with an hour to spare.'

Bern said, 'Take my car.'

'You'd lend me your car?'

'We've saved each other's lives. A car is nothing. But you have another problem.'

'What's that?'

'I was followed here.'

3.00AM: ANTHONY SAT at the wheel of his Cadillac a block from the diner. It appeared to be a cop hangout: two patrol cars were parked outside, along with Billie's red Thunderbird and Bern's Continental.

Ackie Horwitz had been stationed outside Bern Rothsten's apartment. When Bern left in the middle of the night, Ackie had followed. As soon as Bern arrived at the diner, Ackie had alerted Anthony.

Now Ackie came out of the diner. 'Lucas is in there,' he said to

Anthony. 'He has a black coat and a black hat now. Rothsten is with him, and the girl.'

'I'll wait here until Luke comes out, then I'll follow him.'

'Gotcha.' Ackie went to his motorcycle and left.

The door of the diner opened. Billie came out first. The bright lights were behind her, so Anthony could not see her face, but he recognised her small figure. Next came a man in a black coat and black hat: Luke. They went to the red Thunderbird. A man in a trench coat got into the Lincoln. The T-bird moved away, followed by the Lincoln. Anthony waited a few seconds, then pulled out.

Billie headed west, and the Lincoln followed. They came to 14th Street and stopped for a red light. When the light turned green, Billie's Thunderbird suddenly shot forward, while the Lincoln remained stationary. Cursing, Anthony swung round the Lincoln and raced after the others.

Billie zigzagged through the neighbourhood at the back of the White House, shooting red lights, and driving the wrong way on one-way streets. Anthony did the same, but the Cadillac could not match the T-bird for manoeuvrability.

Then luck intervened. Screeching around a corner, Billie ran into a flood. Water was gushing out of a drain and the entire width of the road was two or three inches under. She lost control of her car. The Thunderbird swung round in a wide arc and came to a halt slewed across the street. Anthony pulled across its front, blocking it in. Billie could not get away.

Anthony ran to the passenger side. 'Get out of the car,' he yelled, drawing his gun. The door opened, and the figure in the black coat and hat got out.

Anthony saw immediately that it was not Luke, but Bern. Rage boiled up inside him. 'You idiot!' he screamed at Bern. 'You don't know what you've done!'

'Then tell me, Anthony,' Bern said. 'What have I done?'

Anthony turned away and stuffed the gun back into his coat.

BILLIE LIVED IN ARLINGTON, a leafy suburb on the Virginia side of the Potomac river. Anthony drove along her street. As he passed her house he saw on the other side of the road a Chevrolet belonging to the CIA. He turned a corner and parked.

Billie would be home soon. She knew where Luke had gone but she would not tell Anthony unless he put her under extraordinary pressure. So that was what he would do.

He walked over to the Chevy. 'I'm going in,' he said to Pete. 'Honk if anyone arrives.'

Anthony walked softly up the driveway and went to the back door. He had lived a life of deception and betrayal, but this, he thought with a surge of self-loathing, was the lowest he had ever sunk.

He knew his way around the house. He checked the living room first, then Billie's bedroom. Both were empty. Next he looked in on Becky-Ma. She was fast asleep. Last he went into Larry's room.

He sat on the edge of the bed and switched on the light. 'Hey, Larry, wake up,' he said. 'Come on.'

The boy's eyes opened. After a disorientated moment, he grinned. 'Uncle Anthony,' he said and he smiled.

4.30AM: BILLIE DROPPED Bern off, then drove home.

She entered her house, hung up her coat and went straight upstairs. She kicked off her shoes and went to check on Larry. When she saw his empty bed, she screamed.

She looked into the bathroom, then Becky-Ma's room. 'Larry,' she yelled. 'Where are you?' She ran downstairs and went into every room. She looked in the garage and the yard. Going back inside, she went into every room again, opening closets and checking under beds, looking into every space large enough to hold a seven-year-old. He had gone.

Becky-Ma came out of her bedroom. 'What's happening?' she said shakily.

'Where's Larry?' Billie shouted.

'In his bed, I thought.'

Fighting down panic, Billie went into Larry's bedroom and studied it. The room was tidy, with no signs of struggle. The teddy-bear pyjamas he had worn last night were neatly folded. His school clothes were gone. It looked as if he had gone with someone he trusted. Anthony.

At first she felt relief. Anthony would not harm Larry. But then she thought again. Wouldn't he? She had to get Larry back fast.

She ran downstairs to call Anthony. Before she got to the phone, it rang. She snatched it up. 'Yes?'

'This is Anthony.'

'How could you be so cruel?' she screamed

'I have to know where Luke is,' he said coolly. 'It's important.'

'He's gone—' She stopped herself. 'Where's Larry?'

'He's with me. He's fine, don't worry. Just tell me what I need to know, and everything will be all right.'

'When I see my son, I'll tell you where Luke is.'

'Don't you trust me?'

'Is that a joke?'

He sighed. 'OK. Meet me at the Jefferson Memorial at seven o'clock.'

She checked her watch. It was after six. 'I'll be there.'

She hung up.

'What is it?' Becky-Ma said. 'What's going on?'

Billie tried to give an impression of calm. 'Larry's with Anthony. I'm going to pick him up now.'

She went upstairs. In her bedroom, she stood on a chair and took a small suitcase from on top of the wardrobe. She placed the case on the bed and opened it. Inside was a Colt 45. They had all been issued with Colts in the war. She had kept hers as a souvenir, but some instinct made her clean and oil it regularly. There was a box of bullets in the case. She loaded the gun.

Then she ran out of the house and jumped into her car.

6.30AM: IT WAS STILL DARK when Luke arrived at Newport News and pulled into the parking lot next to the closed airport building. No lights showed except the solitary bulb of a phone booth next to the entrance. He turned off the engine of Bern's Lincoln and listened to the silence. The night was clear and the airfield was starlit.

Luke had been up for more than twenty-four hours, and he felt desperately weary, but his mind was racing. He was in love with Billie. Now that he was two hundred miles away from her, he could admit that to himself. But what about Elspeth? Why had he married her? He had asked Billie that, and she had refused to answer. I'll ask Elspeth, he thought. He checked his watch. He had more than an hour until takeoff. He got out of the car and went to the phone booth.

Elspeth picked up fast, as if she was already awake. Suddenly he felt awkward. 'Uh, good morning, Elspeth.'

'I'm so glad you called,' she said. 'I've been out of my mind with worry. Are you OK?'

'Yes, I'm fine, now. Basically, Anthony caused me to lose my memory, by giving me a combination of electric shock and drugs.'

'Good God. Why would he do a thing like that?'

'He says I'm a Soviet spy.'

'That's absurd.'

'It's what he told Billie.'

'So you've been with Billie?'

Luke heard the note of hostility in Elspeth's voice. 'She's been kind,' he said defensively.

Elspeth changed the subject. 'What are you going to do next?'

'I need to find out what Anthony wanted me to forget.'

'How will you do that?'

'I'd rather not say over the phone.'

'Well, I'm sorry you can't tell me anything.'

'Matter of fact, I called to ask you some things.'

'OK. Fire away.'

'Why can't we have children?'

'We don't know. We've been trying since we got married. Last year, you went to a fertility specialist, but he couldn't find anything wrong. A few weeks ago, I saw a woman doctor in Atlanta. She ran some tests. We're waiting for the results.'

'Would you tell me how we came to get married?'

'Well, I didn't see you for years, then we met again in 1954, in Washington,' she began. 'I was still with the CIA. You were working in Pasadena, but you flew in for Peg's wedding. We were seated together at the breakfast. We talked and talked—it was as if thirteen years had never happened. I had to leave early—I was conductor of the 16th Street Youth Orchestra, and we had a rehearsal. You came with me and afterwards we went back to my place.'

1954: ELSPETH'S APARTMENT was small and uncluttered, with a few pieces of angular modern furniture. Luke made martinis and Elspeth started to cook spaghetti in the tiny kitchen. Luke told her about his job.

'I'm so happy for you,' she said with generous enthusiasm. 'Even back at Harvard, you always wanted to explore outer space.'

He smiled. 'In those days, most people thought it was a foolish dream of science-fiction writers.'

'I guess we still can't be sure it will happen.'

'I think we can,' he said seriously. 'The big problems were solved by German scientists in the war. They built rockets that could be fired in Holland and land on London.'

'I was there, I remember, we called them buzz bombs. So, our missiles are based on the German buzz bombs?'

'More on their V2 rocket, to be exact.'

Luke was not supposed to talk about his work, but this was Elspeth, and anyway she probably had a higher security rating than he did. 'We're building a rocket that can take off in Arizona and explode in Moscow, and if we can do that we can fly to the moon.'

'So it's just the same thing on a larger scale?'

'Yes. We need larger engines, more efficient fuel, that kind of thing. None of these problems is insurmountable. Plus, those German scientists are working for us now.'

'I think I heard that.' She changed the subject. 'And what about life in general?' she asked. 'Are you dating someone?'

'Not right now.' He had dated several girls since his breakup with Billie nine years ago, but none had meant much.

'How about you, Elspeth?' Luke asked. 'Peg's married, Billie's already getting divorced—you've got some catching up to do.'

'Oh, you know about us government girls.' So many young women worked for the government in Washington that they outnumbered single men by five to one. Consequently they were stereotyped as desperate for dates. Luke did not believe Elspeth was like that, but if she wanted to evade his question, she was entitled.

She asked him to watch the stove while she freshened up. He took off his jacket and tie, then stirred the spaghetti sauce.

He heard her call out, 'Luke—could you come here?'

He stepped into the bathroom. Elspeth's dress hung on the back of the door, and she stood in a strapless peach-coloured brassiere and matching half-slip. Her hand was to her face. 'I got soap in my eye, damn it,' she said. 'Would you try to wash it out?'

'Bend down, get your face close to the bowl,' Luke said, encouraging her with his left hand between her shoulder blades. The pale skin of her back was soft and warm to his touch. He cupped water in his right hand and raised it to her eye.

'That helps,' she said.

He rinsed her eye until she said the stinging had stopped. Then he stood her upright and patted her face dry with a clean towel. Her lips parted in a smile. It was the easiest thing in the world to kiss her. She kissed him back, hesitantly at first, then she put her hands behind his neck and pulled his face to hers and kissed him hard.

After a while he picked her up, stepped into the bedroom, and laid her on the bed. When they made love it was slow and intense. 'I've wanted this for so long,' she whispered into his ear; and then she cried out with pleasure, several times, and lay back, exhausted.

Soon Elspeth fell into a deep sleep, but Luke lay awake, thinking about his life. He had always wanted a family, yet here he was, thirty-four and single. Since the war, his career had been his priority, but that was not the real reason he was unmarried. The truth was that only two women had ever touched his heart—Billie and Elspeth. Billie had deceived him, but Elspeth was here beside him.

At daybreak he got up and made coffee. He brought it into the bedroom on a tray, and found Elspeth sitting up in bed, looking sleepily delectable.

'I have something to ask you,' he said taking her hand. 'Will you marry me?'

7.00AM: ANTHONY DROVE up to the Jefferson Memorial with Larry sitting in the front seat between him and Pete. It was still dark, and the area was deserted.

The monument stood on a high platform approached by steps at the rear. 'The statue is nineteen feet high and weighs ten thousand pounds,' he told Larry. 'You can't see it from here, but it's inside those pillars.'

'We should have come in the daytime,' the boy whined.

Anthony had taken Larry out before and they always had a good time. But today Larry knew something was wrong. It was too early and he wanted his mother.

Anthony opened the door. 'Stay here a second, Larry, while I talk to Pete.' The two men got out. Anthony said to Pete, 'I'll wait here. You take the kid and show him the monument. Stay this side, so that she'll see him when she arrives.' He opened the car door again. 'Come on, Larry. Uncle Pete's going to show you the statue.'

Larry got out. With careful politeness, he said, 'After we've seen it, I think I'd like to go home.'

Anthony's breath caught in his throat. Larry's bravery was almost too much. After a moment, Anthony replied in a calm voice, 'We'll check with Mommy. Now go ahead.'

The child took Pete's hand and they walked around the monument towards the steps at the back. A minute later they appeared in front of the pillars, lit by the car's headlights.

Anthony checked his watch. Billie should be here by now. He suffered a pang of doubt. Surely she would come? She was too frightened to call the cops, he felt certain.

He was right. A few moments later, the Thunderbird arrived. It parked twenty yards from Anthony's Cadillac and a small, slight figure jumped out, leaving the engine running.

'Hello, Billie,' said Anthony.

She looked from him to the monument and saw Pete and Larry up on the raised platform.

Anthony walked towards her. 'Don't try anything dramatic—it would upset Larry.'

'Don't talk to me about upsetting him, you son of a bitch.' Her voice cracked with strain. She was near to tears.

'I had to do this.'

'Nobody *has* to do something like this.'

It was a waste of time arguing with her. 'Where's Luke?' he said abruptly.

After a pause she said, 'Luke caught a plane to Huntsville.'

Anthony breathed a deep sigh. He had what he needed. 'Why Huntsville?' he asked. 'Why not Florida?'

'I don't know why.'

Anthony tried to read her face, but it was too dark. 'You're holding something back.'

'I don't care what you think. I'm going to take my son and leave.'

'No, you're not. We're keeping him for a while.'

Billie's voice was a cry of anguish. 'Why? I've told you where Luke went!'

'There may be other ways you can help us.'

'No. It's not fair!'

'You'll live.' He turned away. That was his mistake.

Billie had been half expecting this. As he stepped towards his car, she rushed him. With her right shoulder, she hit him in the small of the back. She weighed only 120 pounds, but she had surprise and rage on her side. He stumbled and fell forward, coming down on his hands and knees.

Billie took the Colt 45 from her coat pocket. As Anthony tried to get up, she dropped to one knee and shoved the barrel of the gun into his mouth. She felt a tooth break.

'I'm going to take the gun out of your mouth,' she said. 'You're going to call to your colleague and tell him what I say.' She took the gun out of Anthony's mouth and pointed it at his left eye. 'Now,' she said. 'Call him.'

Anthony hesitated. She touched the barrel of the pistol to his eyelid.

'Pete!' he shouted.

Pete looked round. 'Where are you?' he said. Anthony and Billie were outside the range of the headlights.

Billie pressed the gun into Anthony's eye. 'Tell him to stay there.'

Anthony shouted, 'Stay where you are!'

'What's happening?' Pete called. 'I can't see you.'

Billie shouted, 'Larry, this is Mom. Get in the T-bird!'

Pete grabbed Larry's arm.

'Uncle Anthony's going to tell the man to let you go.' She pressed the gun barrel harder into Anthony's eye.

'Let the kid go!' Anthony shouted. 'She's got a gun on me!'

'OK!' Pete released Larry's arm.

Larry ran towards Billie. 'Not this way,' she said, struggling to keep her voice calm. 'Get in the car, quickly.'

Larry ran to the Thunderbird and jumped in.

With a lashing movement, Billie hit Anthony on both sides of his face with the gun, as hard as she could. He lay still, groaning. She said, 'Remember that if you're ever tempted to kidnap a child again.'

She backed towards her car, keeping the gun on him. She glanced up at the monument. Pete had not moved.

She got into her car and stuffed the Colt inside her jacket. 'Are you OK?' she asked Larry.

He started to cry. She shoved the gearshift into first and tore away.

8.00AM: BERN POURED warm milk over Larry's cornflakes while Billie beat up an egg for French toast. They were giving their child comfort food, but Billie felt the adults needed comfort too.

'I'm going to kill that son of a bitch Anthony,' Bern muttered, speaking quietly so that Larry would not hear.

Billie's rage had evaporated. Now she was worried and frightened. 'I'm afraid Anthony may try to kill Luke. I didn't think it was possible, a few hours ago—but now I know better.'

Bern dipped a slice of white bread into the egg mixture. 'Luke won't kill easy.'

'But he thinks he's escaped—he doesn't know I've told Anthony where he is. I have to find a way to warn him.'

'Leave a message at the Huntsville airport?'

'It's not reliable enough. I think I have to go there myself.'

Billie picked up the airline guide. Flight 271 left Washington at exactly nine, landing at Huntsville four minutes before noon. Luke's flight did not land until two twenty-three. 'I can do it,' she said, but she hesitated, looking at Larry.

'He'll be OK. I'll take care of him.'

Bern was a trained agent and could protect his kid from just about anything. Billie made a decision. She would go to Huntsville.

'Mommy has to go now,' she said to Larry. 'You have a fun day with Daddy and maybe he'll take you swimming.'

'OK.'

She did not want to make a drama of saying goodbye, for that would scare the child. 'I'll see you later,' she said casually.

As she went out, she heard Bern say, 'I bet you couldn't eat a slice of French toast.'

'I could too,' Larry replied.

Part Five

10.45am: Luke's plane refuelled at Winston-Salem, and the passengers got off for a few minutes. Luke called Redstone Arsenal from the terminal and got Marigold on the phone.

'Dr Lucas!' she said. 'Are you OK?'

'I'm fine, but I only have a minute or two. Is the launch still scheduled for tonight?'

'Yes, ten thirty.'

'I'm on my way to Huntsville—my plane lands at two twenty-three. I'm trying to figure out why I went there on Monday. Do you have any idea what I did there?'

'Well, now, let me see. I met you at the airport in an army car and brought you here to the base. You went into the Computation Lab, then drove yourself down to the south end.'

'What's there, at the south end?'

'The Engineering Building—you sometimes work there.'

'And then?'

'You asked me to drive you home. I waited in the car while you stepped inside for a minute or two. Then I took you to the airport.'

Desperately, Luke cast about for another line of questioning. 'When you met me, was I carrying anything?'

'Just your little suitcase. Oh, and a file.'

'A file?' he said. He swallowed. 'Was it any special kind of file?'

'A standard army file folder, thin cardboard, buff-coloured.'

'And did I still have this file when you took me to the airport?'

A stewardess interrupted. 'Time to board the aircraft, Dr Lucas.'

'I'm coming, I'm coming.' He repeated his question to Marigold.

'I'm trying to remember. You know, I don't believe you had it at the airport.'

'Are you sure?'

'Yes. You must have left that file either at the base or at home.'

Luke's mind was racing. The file was the reason for his trip to Huntsville, he felt sure. It contained the secret he had found out, the one that Anthony was so desperate for him to forget. He had stashed it somewhere for safekeeping. Now, if he could find it, he could discover the secret.

'I think that file could be very important. Could you look around and see if it's there?'

'My lord, Dr Lucas, this is the army! Don't you know there must be a million of them buff-coloured file folders here?'

'Just check around. As soon as I land at Huntsville, I'll go to the house and search there. Then, if I don't find it, I'll come to the base.'

Luke hung up and ran for the plane. Its propellers were already turning.

11.00AM: THE MATS FLIGHT to Huntsville was full of generals. MATS was the Military Air Transport Service. Anthony wore sunglasses to conceal the two black eyes Billie had given him. His lip had stopped bleeding, and the broken tooth showed only when he talked.

Should he simply take the first opportunity to kill Luke? It was temptingly simple. But he worried that he did not know exactly what Luke was up to. He had to make a decision. However, by the time he boarded the plane he had been awake for forty-eight hours straight, and he fell asleep. Next thing he knew, Pete was shaking him awake, as a corporal opened the aircraft door. Huntsville had a civilian airport, but MATS flights came down on the airstrip within Redstone Arsenal.

'I'm going to make some enquiries at the base,' he said to Pete. 'I want you to go to the airport and keep watch. If Luke arrives, try to reach me there.'

At the edge of the airstrip, a young man in the uniform of a lieutenant waited with a card that read: MR CARROLL, STATE DEPARTMENT. Anthony shook his hand. 'Colonel Hickam's compliments, sir,' the lieutenant said and pointed to an olive-drab Ford.

'That'll be fine,' Anthony said. He had called the base before catching his plane, brazenly pretending he was under orders from CIA Director Alan Dulles.

'Colonel Hickam would be glad if you would drop by headquarters at your convenience.' The lieutenant handed Anthony a map. 'The headquarters building is marked on the map. And we have a message, asking you to call Mr Carl Hobart in Washington.'

'Thank you, lieutenant. Where's Dr Claude Lucas's office?'

'That'll be the Computation Laboratory.' He took out a pencil and made a mark on the map.

'Does Dr Lucas have a secretary?'

'Yes—Mrs Marigold Clarke.'

'Lieutenant, this is my colleague Pete Maxell. If he needs to reach me here at the base, what's the best way?'

The lieutenant looked at Pete. 'Sir, you could always leave a message at Colonel Hickam's office, and I would try to get it to Mr Carroll.'

'Good enough,' Anthony said, and got into the Ford. He checked the map, and started out. It was a typical army base. Arrow-straight roads ran through rough woodland broken by neat rectangles of lawn close-cropped like a conscript's haircut. The buildings were all flat-roofed structures of tan brick. He easily found the Computation Lab.

He went into the building. In an outer office were three small desks. Two were vacant. The third was occupied by a Negro woman of about fifty. 'Good afternoon,' he said.

She looked up. 'Hello! How can I help you?'

'I'm from Colonel Hickam's office,' he said. 'I'm looking for Marigold Clark.'

'That's me.'

'I guess you know that Dr Lucas is on his way here.'

'He called me this morning. His plane lands at two twenty-three.'

That was useful. 'So he'll be here around three?'

'Not necessarily. He said he's going home first.'

That was perfect. Anthony could hardly believe his luck. He could go there and wait, then shoot Luke as soon as he walked in the door. With Elspeth in Florida, the corpse might not be found for days.

'Thank you,' he said to Marigold. He left the room before she could ask his name.

He returned to the car and drove to the headquarters building. He found Colonel Hickam's office. The colonel was out, but a sergeant showed him to an empty room with a phone.

He called Q Building, but did not speak to his boss, Carl Hobart. Instead he asked for Carl's superior, George Cooperman.

'Did you shoot at someone last night?' asked Cooperman.

With an effort, Anthony put on the swashbuckling persona that appealed to Cooperman. 'Aw, hell, who told you that?'

'Some colonel from the Pentagon called Tom Ealy in the Director's office, and Ealy told Carl Hobart.'

'There's no proof, I picked up all the slugs.'

'This colonel found a hole in the wall about nine millimetres wide and he guessed what caused it. Did you hit anybody?'

'Unfortunately not.'

'You're supposed to come back immediately.'

'Then it's a good thing I didn't talk to you.'

'Listen, Anthony, I always cut you as much slack as I can, because you get results. But I can't do any more for you on this one. You're on your own from here, buddy.'

'That's how I like it.'

'Good luck.'

Anthony sat staring at the phone. He could disobey orders for only so long. He needed to wrap this up fast.

He called Elspeth. 'Have you talked to Luke?' he asked her.

'He called me at six thirty this morning.' She sounded shaky. 'He wouldn't say where he was going or what he intended to do. But he knows you were responsible for his amnesia.'

'He's on his way to Huntsville. I'm at Redstone Arsenal now. I'm going to your house to wait for him there. Will I be able to get in?'

She answered with another question. 'Are you still trying to protect him?'

'Of course.'

There was a moment's pause, then she said, 'There's a key under the bougainvillea pot in the back yard. Take care of Luke, won't you?'

'I'll do my best.' He hung up.

As he stood up to go, the phone rang.

Only Pete knew he was in Colonel Hickam's office. He picked up.

It was Pete. 'Dr Josephson's here,' he said. 'She just got off a plane. She's sitting in the terminal, like she's waiting.'

'Damn her. She's come to warn him that we're here. You have to get her out of there.'

'How?'

'I don't care—just get rid of her!'

12 NOON: HUNTSVILLE AIRPORT was small but busy. As soon as she arrived, Billie checked on Luke's flight and learned it was running almost an hour late. She had three hours to kill.

A girl in a Capital Airlines uniform approached her. 'Are you Dr Josephson?'

'Yes.'

'I have a phone message for you.' She handed over an envelope.

Billie tore open the envelope and read: *Please call Dr Lucas on Huntsville JE 6-4231.*

She was bewildered. Could Luke be here already? There was only one way to find out. She found a payphone and dialled the number. A man's voice answered: 'Components test lab.'

'Dr Claude Lucas, please.'

'Just one moment.' After a pause the man came back. 'Dr Lucas stepped out for a minute. Who is this, please?'

'Dr Bilhah Josephson, I have a message to call him.'

'Oh, Dr Josephson, I'm so glad we found you! Dr Lucas is very concerned to contact you.'

'What's he doing here? I thought he was still in the air.'

'Army security pulled him off the plane at Norfolk, Virginia, and laid on a special flight. He's been here more than an hour. Can you get yourself down to us?'

'Where are you?'

'The lab is about an hour out of town on the Chattanooga road.'

Billie took a notebook out of her bag. 'Give me directions.'

3.00PM: BILLIE WAS LOST. Leaving the airport in a rented Ford a few minutes before one o'clock, she had driven into the centre of Huntsville then taken Highway 59 towards Chattanooga. She had wondered why the components testing laboratory was an hour away from the base, and imagined it might be for safety reasons.

The landscape gradually became wilder and the roads narrower. The disparity between what she expected and the landmarks she saw around her grew until she threw up her hands in despair. She was furious with herself and with the fool who had given her directions.

After a couple of miles, she came upon a dilapidated feed store with a payphone outside. She pulled over. She still had Luke's message with the phone number. She put a dime in the slot and dialled. The phone was answered immediately.

'May I speak to Dr Claude Lucas?' she said.

'You got the wrong number, honey.'

'Isn't this Huntsville JE 6-4231?'

'Yep. You've reached a payphone in Huntsville airport.'

'A *pay*phone?'

'Yes, ma'am.'

Billie realised she had been hoodwinked. Luke had not been taken off his plane in Norfolk and put on an army flight. That whole story was a lie designed to get her out of the way. With despair in her heart, she wondered if he were still alive. If he was, maybe she could still warn him. She racked her brains. Luke had a secretary at the base, she remembered; a name like a flower . . . Marigold.

She called Redstone Arsenal and asked to speak to Dr Lucas's secretary. A woman with a slow Alabama voice came on the line.

'Is that Marigold?'

'Yes.'

'I'm Dr Josephson, a friend of Dr Lucas. We've spoken before, I think. My name is Billie.'

'Oh, sure, I remember. How are you?'

'Worried. I need to get a message to Luke urgently. Is he with you?'

'No, ma'am. He went to his house.'

'If you see Luke, or if he calls you, would you give him a message from me? Tell him Anthony is in town. He'll understand.'

'I'll do that, Doctor.'

'Thank you.' Billie hung up.

Was there anyone else Luke might talk to? She thought of Elspeth. She called the operator and asked for Cape Canaveral.

3.45PM: EVERYONE WAS bad-tempered at Cape Canaveral. The Pentagon had ordered a security alert. Arriving for work in the morning, staff had been made to wait in line at the gate. Cars had been searched, briefcases opened and lunch pails unpacked. Elspeth was glad of the upset. It meant that nobody noticed she was too distraught to do her job. She did not know where Luke was and she no longer felt sure she could trust Anthony.

When the phone at her desk rang a few minutes before four o'clock, her heart seemed to stop. She snatched up the handset. 'Yes?'

'This is Billie.'

'Billie?' Elspeth was taken by surprise. 'Where are you?'

'I'm in Huntsville, trying to contact Luke.'

'What's he doing there?'

'Looking for a file he left here on Monday.'

'He went to Huntsville on Monday? I didn't know that.'

'Nobody knew, except Marigold. Elspeth, do you understand what's going on?'

She laughed humourlessly. 'I thought I did, but not any more.'

'I believe Luke's life is in danger. Anthony shot at him in Washington last night.'

Elspeth went cold. 'Oh, my God.'

'It's too complicated to explain right now. If Luke calls you, will you tell him that Anthony is in Huntsville?'

Elspeth was trying to recover from the shock. 'Of course I will. Billie . . . one more thing. Look after Luke, won't you?'

'What do you mean?' Billie asked. 'You sound like you're going to die.'

Elspeth did not answer. After a moment she broke the connection. A sob came to her throat. She fought fiercely to control herself. Then she dialled her home in Huntsville.

4.00PM: ANTHONY LOOKED out of the front window of Luke's house and saw a Huntsville taxicab pull up at the kerb. He thumbed the safety catch on his gun. His mouth went dry,

The phone rang. He was paralysed by indecision. He looked out of the window and saw Luke getting out of the cab. The call could be trivial or it could be vital information.

He snatched the phone up. 'Yes?'

'This is Elspeth.' Her voice was low. 'He's looking for a file he stashed in Huntsville on Monday.'

Anthony understood in a flash. Luke had copied the blueprints he had brought to Washington. He had made a clandestine stop in Huntsville to hide the copies.

'Who else knows about this?'

'His secretary, Marigold. And Billie—she told me. Maybe others.'

Luke was paying the driver. Anthony was running out of time. 'I have to have that file,' he said to Elspeth.

'That's what I thought.'

'It's not here,' he said. 'I just searched the house.'

'Then it must be at the base.'

'I'll have to follow him while he looks for it.'

Luke was approaching the front door.

'I'm out of time,' Anthony said, and he slammed down the phone.

He heard the key scrape in the lock as he ran through the hall and into the kitchen. He went out of the back door and closed it softly. He slipped the key under the flowerpot.

He reached the street and walked away.

4:30PM: ON TOP OF THE TV in the living room was a bamboo picture frame containing a photograph of a beautiful redhead in an ivory silk wedding dress. Beside her, wearing a grey cutaway, was Luke. He studied Elspeth in the picture. She could have been a movie star.

Luke began to search. A buff-coloured file folder should be easy enough to find. He sat at the desk in the study and looked through the drawers. He found nothing.

Upstairs he opened the closet and saw, with pleasure, the rack of navy blue and grey suits and tweed sports jackets. He had been wearing this stolen suit for more than twenty-four hours, and he was tempted to take five minutes to shower and change into some of his own clothes. But he resisted. There was no time to spare.

He searched the house thoroughly. Everywhere he looked, he learned something about himself and his wife. They liked Glen Miller and Frank Sinatra, they read Hemingway and Scott Fitzgerald, they drank Dewar's Scotch and ate All-Bran.

At last he gave up. In a kitchen drawer he found keys to the black Chrysler in the garage. He would drive to the base and search there.

Before leaving, he picked up the mail in the hall and shuffled the envelopes. Desperate for a clue, he ripped them open. One was from a doctor in Atlanta.

> Dear Mrs Lucas,
>
> Following your routine checkup, the results of your blood tests have come back from the lab, and everything is normal. However, you are under weight, you suffer insomnia, and when I saw you, you had obviously been crying. These are symptoms of depression. Depression may be caused by changes in body chemistry, by unresolved mental problems such as marital difficulties, or by childhood trauma such as the early death of a parent. In your case, I have no doubt that the condition is related to the tubal ligation you underwent in 1954.

Luke stopped reading. Tubal ligation was a method of sterilisation. When he had asked Elspeth why they could not have children, she had said, 'We don't know. We've been trying since we got married.' That was all lies. She knew perfectly well why they could not have children: she had been sterilised. He looked at the next paragraph.

> This procedure may cause depression at any age, but in your case, having it six weeks before your wedding—

Luke's mouth fell open. Elspeth's deception had begun shortly before they got married. Their marriage had been a lie. He had wanted children—yet children were the very thing she had deliberately denied him. And she had lied about it for four years.

He stepped into his study and sat at his desk, staring through the window, while evening fell over the hickory trees in the back yard. How had he let his life go so wrong? He must be a poor judge of people, he thought. He had remained close to Anthony, who had tried to kill him, yet had broken with Bern who had been a faithful friend. He had quarrelled with Billie and married Elspeth, yet Billie had dropped everything to help him, and Elspeth had deceived him.

A large moth bumped into the window, and startled Luke out of his reverie. He looked at his watch and was shocked to see that it was past seven. If he hoped to unravel the mystery of his life, he needed to start with the mysterious file. It was not here, so it had to be at Redstone Arsenal. Time was pressing. The launch of the rocket was scheduled for ten thirty. He had only three hours to find out whether there was a plot to sabotage it.

7.30PM: THERE WERE NO LIGHTS on in Luke's house when Billie drove by. It had taken her hours to get back to Huntsville and find the house. She had no idea whether either of her warning messages had reached Luke. She was furious with herself for being so incompetent.

She turned the next corner and pulled up. She breathed deeply and made herself think calmly. She had to find out what was in the house. But what if Anthony were there? On the passenger seat beside her was an attaché case. She opened it up and took out her Colt. Then she turned the car around and returned to Luke's house.

She parked outside, grabbed her gun and leaped out. She jumped the low wall and ran across the lawn to the side of the house.

She heard no sound from within. She ran round to the back and looked in at a window. The room seemed empty. She reversed her grip on the gun and smashed the glass. She reached through the broken pane, undid the latch and opened the window.

She climbed in and moved through the house in the gloom, dreading at every step that she would see Luke on the floor. All the rooms were empty. Had Luke changed his mind and decided not to come here? Or had the body been spirited away? Had Anthony somehow failed to kill him? Or had one of her warnings got through?

One person who might have some answers was Marigold.

She found a phone and called information. She asked for a number for Marigold Clark. After a moment the voice on the line gave her a Huntsville number.

A man answered. 'She's at choir practice at the Calvary Gospel Church on Mill Street.'

Billie went out to her car. She found Mill Street on the Hertz map and drove there. The church was a fine brick building in a poor neighbourhood. There were only about thirty men and women in the choir, but they sounded like a hundred. They clapped and swayed as they sang, and a large woman with her back to Billie conducted vigorously.

They finished on a high chord, and the conductor looked around and saw her. 'Take a short break,' she said to the choir.

'I'm sorry to interrupt,' Billie said. 'Are you Marigold Clark?'

'Yes,' the woman said warily. 'But I don't know you.'

'We spoke on the phone earlier, I'm Billie Josephson.'

'Oh, hi, Dr Josephson.'

Billie said, 'Have you heard from Luke?'

'Not since this morning. I expected him to show up at the base, but he didn't. Do you think he's all right?'

'I don't know. I went to his house, but there was no one there. I'm afraid he might have been killed.'

Marigold shook her head in bewilderment. 'I've worked for the army twenty years and I never heard of anything like this.'

'He's in great danger.' Billie looked Marigold in the eye. 'Do you believe me?'

Marigold hesitated for a long moment. 'Yes, I do,' she said at last.

'Then you have to help me,' Billie told her.

9.30PM: ANTHONY WAS at Redstone Arsenal, sitting in his army Ford, watching the door of the Computation Laboratory. Luke was in the lab, searching for his file folder. Anthony knew he would not find it there, because he had already searched there.

Time was on Anthony's side. Every minute that passed made Luke less dangerous. The rocket would be launched in one hour. Could Luke ruin everything in an hour?

The door to the lab opened. Luke emerged and approached the black Chrysler parked at the kerb. He got in and drove off. Anthony switched on his headlights, and followed.

After about a mile, Luke slowed in front of a long one-storey building and pulled into its parking lot.

LUKE HAD FELT SURE he would find the folder in the Computation Lab, where his office was, but he found nothing. There was one more possibility. Marigold had said that he also went to the Engineering Building on Monday.

Engineering had an atmosphere quite different from that of the Computation Lab. Computation was spotlessly clean for the sake of the massive computers. Engineering was scruffy by comparison, smelling of oil and rubber.

Luke hurried along a corridor. At the end he came upon a large room with half a dozen steel tables. On the far side, an open door led into a laboratory. Along the wall to his left was a row of lockers, each with a name plate. One was his. Maybe he had stashed the file here.

The cupboard was locked. He took out his key ring and found a likely key. It worked, and he opened the door. Inside was a hard hat on a high shelf. Below that, hanging from a hook, were blue overalls, and on the floor, a pair of black rubber boots.

There, beside the boots, was a buff-coloured army file folder. This had to be what he was looking for.

The folder contained a large brown envelope, already open. Inside were some papers. When he took them out, he could see immediately that they were blueprints for parts of a rocket. He moved quickly to one of the steel tables and spread the papers out under a lamp. After a few moments' rapid study, he knew without doubt that the drawings showed the Jupiter-C rocket's self-destruct mechanism.

He was horrified.

Every rocket had a self-destruct mechanism so that, if it should veer off course and threaten human life, it could be blown up in midair. The explosion was triggered by a coded radio signal. An igniter rope ran the length of the rocket's main stage. At its top end was a firing cap with two wires sticking out. If a voltage was applied across the wires, the cap would ignite the rope, which would rip open the fuel tank and destroy the rocket. The blueprints showed twin plugs, one for the transmitter on the ground and the other for the receiver in the satellite. One turned the radio signal into a complex code; the other received the signal and applied the voltage across the two wires.

A separate diagram, not a blueprint but a hastily drawn sketch, showed exactly how the plugs were wired, so that anyone having the diagram could duplicate the signal. It was brilliant, Luke realised. The saboteurs had no need of explosives or timing devices, nor did they need access to the rocket. The radio signal could be broadcast from a transmitter miles away.

Written on the envelope were the words: *Theo Packman, Vanguard Motel*. Presumably Packman was, even now, somewhere in Cocoa Beach with a radio transmitter, ready to blow up the rocket seconds after it took off. But now Luke could prevent that. It was ten fifteen. He had time to call Cape Canaveral and have the launch postponed. He snatched up the phone.

A voice said, 'Put it down, Luke.' Luke turned slowly. Anthony stood in the doorway pointing a gun at Luke.

Luke stared at the man whom he had so misjudged. 'How long have you been working for Moscow?' Luke asked him. 'Since the war?'

'Longer. Since Harvard.'

'Why?'

Anthony's lips twisted into a strange smile. 'For a better world.'

Once upon a time, Luke knew, a lot of sensible people had believed in the Soviet system, but their faith had been undermined by the realities of life under Stalin. 'You still believe that?' he said.

'Sort of. It's still the best hope, despite all that has happened.'

'But you shot at me last night. Would you kill your oldest friend for a cause you only half believe in?'

'Yes, and so would you. In the war we both put lives at risk, our own and other people's, because it was right.'

'I don't think we lied to one another, let alone shot at one another.'

'We would have, if necessary. And if I don't kill you now, you'll try to stop me escaping—won't you? Even though you know that if I'm caught I'll finish up in the electric chair.'

'I guess so . . . yes.'

'So you're willing to kill a friend, too.'

Luke was taken aback. Surely he could not be classified with Anthony? 'I might bring you to justice. That's not murder.'

'I'd be just as dead, though.'

Luke nodded slowly. 'I guess you would.'

Anthony raised the gun with a steady hand, aiming at Luke's heart.

Luke dropped behind the steel table. The silenced gun coughed, and there was a metallic clang as the bullet hit the top of the table.

Luke rolled under the table and he lifted himself into a stoop, so that his back was against the underside of the table. Grabbing the two legs at one end he heaved, standing upright at the same time. The table came up off the floor and teetered forward. Luke ran blindly with it, hoping to collide with Anthony. The table crashed to the floor, but Anthony was not beneath it.

Luke tripped and fell, banging his head on a steel leg. He rolled sideways and came up into a sitting position, hurt and dazed. He looked up to see Anthony facing him, braced with his feet apart, aiming his gun two-handed. Luke was now, literally, a sitting target.

Then a voice rang out: 'Anthony! Stop!' It was Billie.

Anthony froze. Luke slowly turned his head. Billie stood by the door, holding an automatic pistol, levelled at Anthony. Behind her was a middle-aged Negro woman, looking shocked and scared.

'Drop the gun!' Billie yelled.

Slowly, Anthony lowered his arms, but he did not drop the gun.

'Drop it, or I'll shoot!'

Anthony smiled. 'No, you won't,' he said. Still pointing the gun at the floor, he began to walk backwards, making for the open door that led into the laboratory. 'You don't believe that a rocket is worth more than a human life, even if it's a traitor's life.'

'Don't test me!' Billie cried.

Anthony turned and darted through the doorway.

Luke leaped to his feet. The clock on the wall said ten

twenty-nine. He had a minute left to warn Cape Canaveral. He picked up the phone. 'This is Luke,' he said. 'Give me the launch conductor. Put him on, quick!'

There was a pause. In the background, Luke could hear the countdown in the blockhouse: 'Twenty, nineteen, eighteen—'

A new voice came on the line. 'This is Willy—what the hell is it?'

'Someone has the self-destruct code. They're going to blow up the rocket. You have to abort the launch.'

The background voice said, 'Eleven, ten—'

'How do you know?' Willy asked.

'I've found diagrams of the wiring of the coded plugs, and an envelope addressed to someone called Theo Packman.'

'That's not proof. I can't cancel the launch on that.'

Luke suddenly felt fatalistic. 'I've told you what I know. The decision is yours.'

'Five, four—'

'Hell,' Willy raised his voice. 'Stop the countdown!'

Luke glanced up at the anxious faces of Billie and Marigold. 'They've aborted the launch.'

A new voice came on the line. 'Luke? This is Colonel Hide. What the hell is going on?'

'I've discovered what made me take off for Washington in such a hurry on Monday. Do you know who Theo Packman is?'

'Yeah, he's a freelance journalist on the missile beat.'

'I found an envelope addressed to him containing blueprints of the Jupiter's self-destruct system. That's why I persuaded Willy to abort the launch.'

'Thank God you did.'

'Listen, you have to find this Packman character right now. The envelope was addressed to the Vanguard Motel.'

'Got it.'

'Packman was working with someone in the CIA, a double agent called Anthony Carroll. He's the one who intercepted me in Washington before I could get to the Pentagon with the information.'

'I'll call the CIA and tell them.'

Luke hung up the phone and sat back. He had done all he could.

He looked at Billie, who said, 'What next?'

'I guess I'll go to Cape Canaveral. The launch will be rescheduled for the same time tomorrow. I'd like to be there.'

'Me, too.'

Luke smiled. 'You deserve it. You saved the rocket.' He stood up and embraced her.

'Your life, you idiot. To heck with the rocket, I saved your life.' She kissed him.

Marigold coughed. 'You've missed the last plane from Huntsville airport,' she said in a businesslike tone. 'Next one is a MATS flight that leaves at five thirty in the morning. Or there's a train. It stops in Chattanooga around one o'clock tonight. You could get there in a couple of hours by car.'

Billie said, 'I like the train idea.'

They said goodbye to Marigold, who offered to return Billie's rental to Hertz, got into Luke's Chrysler and drove away.

When they were on the highway, Billie said to Luke, 'There's a question we haven't talked about.'

'I know,' he said. 'Who sent the blueprints to Theo Packman?'

'It must be someone inside Cape Canaveral, someone on the scientific team.'

'Exactly.'

'Do you have any idea who?'

With a heart full of grief, Luke said, 'I think it's Elspeth.'

11.00PM: ELSPETH COULD NOT believe it. Just a few seconds before ignition, the launch had been postponed. The triumph of her life had been within her grasp—and had slipped through her fingers.

She was on the flat roof of an administration building, with a small crowd of secretaries and clerks, watching the floodlit launch pad through binoculars. Their fears had grown as the minutes ticked by and the rocket remained on the ground, and now a collective groan went up as technicians in overalls swarmed out of their bunkers and began to the complex procedure of standing down all systems.

Elspeth left the others without a word and walked back to Hangar R. When she reached her office, the phone was ringing. She snatched it up. 'Yes?'

'What's happening?' The voice was Anthony's.

'They've aborted the launch. I don't know why—do you?'

'Luke found the papers. He must have called.'

'Couldn't you stop him?'

'I had him in my sights—literally—but Billie walked in, armed.'

'Is Luke all right?'

'Yes, but Theo's name is on those papers. They'll be on their way to arrest him. You have to find him first.'

'Let me think . . . he's on the beach. I know his car, it's a Hudson Hornet.'

'Then get going!'

She slammed down the phone and rushed out of the building. She ran across the parking lot and jumped into her white Corvette.

There was no regular road to the beach. From the highway several tracks led between the dunes to the shore. She planned to take the first, then continue south on the beach. That way she could not miss Theo's car. She had to go slowly for fear of missing the turn-off in the dark. Then she saw a car emerging. It was followed by another, and another. Elspeth flashed her left-turn indicator. A constant stream of cars was coming from the beach. The spectators had figured out that the launch was cancelled and they were all going home.

A car behind her honked impatiently. She saw she was not going to be able to get to the beach this way. Could she wait on the highway in the hope of spotting his car? It was too chancy. Her best option was to go to his motel and wait there.

She sped on. She wondered if Army security was already at the Vanguard Motel. She had a chance of beating them if she hurried.

The Vanguard had a large parking lot out front. There was no sign of police or army security: she was in time. But Theo's car was not here. She parked near the motel office.

She did not have to wait long. The yellow-and-brown Hudson Hornet pulled in a couple of minutes later. Theo eased into a slot at the far end of the lot, and got out, a small man with thinning hair, dressed in chinos and a beach shirt.

Elspeth got out of her car. She opened her mouth to call to him. At that moment, two police cruisers arrived. They came in fast, but without flashing lights or sirens. Behind them followed two unmarked cars. They parked across the entry making it impossible for cars to leave.

Theo did not see them. He headed towards the motel office. Elspeth knew in a flash what she had to do. She took a deep breath, then started walking towards him. As he came close he recognised her and said loudly, 'What the hell happened to the launch?'

Elspeth said in a low voice, 'Give me your car keys.'

'What for?'

'Look behind you.'

He glanced over his shoulder and saw the police cars.

'Stay calm. Give me the keys.' He dropped them into her open hand. 'Keep walking,' she said. 'The trunk of my car is not locked. Get inside.' She went on past him.

Elspeth recognised Colonel Hide and another vaguely familiar face from Cape Canaveral. With them were four local cops and two tall, well-dressed men who might have been FBI agents.

She reached Theo's car and opened the trunk. Inside was the suitcase containing the radio transmitter—powerful, and heavy. She dragged it over the lip of the trunk. It hit the ground with a thud. She closed the trunk lid quickly.

She looked around. At the other end of the lot, she saw the trunk of her own car slowly closing, as if of its own volition. Theo was inside. Gritting her teeth, she grasped the handle of the suitcase and lifted. It felt like a box of lead. She walked a few yards, then dropped it. She picked it up with her other hand. She managed another ten yards before she dropped the case again.

Behind her, Colonel Hide and his men were crossing the lot towards the motel office. She prayed Hide would not look at her face. The darkness made it less likely he would recognise her.

Giving up carrying the transmitter, she began to drag it across the concrete, hoping the noise would not attract the attention of the cops.

At last she reached her car. As she opened the trunk, one of the uniformed police approached her with a cheerful smile. 'Help you with that, ma'am?' he said politely.

Theo's face stared at her from inside the trunk, white and scared.

'I got it,' she said. With both hands, she heaved up the suitcase and slid it in. There was a quiet grunt of pain from Theo as a corner dug into him. Quickly, Elspeth slammed the trunk lid. 'Thanks, anyway.'

'Checking out?' the cop said.

'Yeah.'

He bent, looked into the car, then straightened up. 'Drive safely.'

Elspeth got into her car and started the engine.

The cop went to one of the cruisers and moved it out of the way.

She drove through the gap and pulled onto the highway, then floored the gas pedal.

1.00AM: THE TRAIN PULLED out of Chattanooga. In the cramped roomette, Luke took off his jacket and hung it up, then perched on the edge of the lower bunk and unlaced his shoes. Billie sat watching him. Luke undid his tie and Billie said, 'If this is a striptease, it doesn't have much oomph.'

Luke grinned ruefully. They had been forced to share the roomette: only one was available. He was longing to take Billie in his arms, yet he hesitated.

'What?' she said. 'What are you thinking?'

'That this is too quick.'

'Seventeen years is nothing?'

'To me it's been a couple of days, that's all I can remember. And I'm still married to Elspeth.'

Billie nodded solemnly. 'But she's been lying to you for years.'

'I don't like the feeling that I'm seizing an excuse.' She said nothing in reply, so he added, 'You don't agree, do you?'

'No, I want to make love to you tonight, but I know you. You've never been one to live for the moment, even when we were kids.'

'Is that so bad?'

'No. I'm glad you're like that. It makes you rock-solid reliable. If you weren't this way, I guess I wouldn't have . . .' Her voice tailed off.

'What were you going to say?'

She looked him in the eye. 'I wouldn't have loved you this much, this long.' She was embarrassed, and covered up by saying 'Why don't you climb up on top, and give me room to take off my shoes.'

Obediently, he climbed the ladder and lay down on the top bunk.

She kicked off her shoes and stood up. She slipped off her black ski pants and stood there in her sweater and panties. Catching his eye, she grinned and said, 'It's OK, you can watch.' She reached under her sweater at the back and unfastened her brassiere. Then she drew her left arm out of her sleeve and drew her bra out of her right sleeve with a conjurer's flourish.

'Bravo,' he said.

She stood on the edge of the lower bunk and raised herself to his level, tilting her face to be kissed. He touched her lips with his own. Then she pulled away.

He lay thinking about her lying a few inches below, with her bare legs and her round breasts inside the soft angora sweater. In a few moments he was asleep.

He had an intensely erotic dream and woke up slowly, reluctant to return to the world of rockets and treachery. His shirt was open and his pants were undone. Billie lay beside him, kissing him. 'Are you awake? I don't want to waste this on a guy who's asleep.'

He ran his hand along her side. 'I'm awake,' he said thickly.

He felt as if he were still half in the dream, as the train rocked and Billie kissed him and America flew by the window mile after mile. He wound his arms around her back and held her tightly, to convince himself that she was real, not a fantasy. Just as he was thinking that he wanted this to go on for ever, his body took control, and he clung to her as waves of pleasure broke over him.

Part Six

8.30am: Anthony flew to Florida in a small MATS plane that bumped and bucked with every gust of wind all the way across Alabama and Georgia. The CIA did not yet believe he was a double agent. He was accompanied by a general and two colonels who would have shot him on sight if they had known the purpose of his trip.

He landed at Patrick Air Force base, a few miles south of Cape Canaveral. In his imagination he saw a detachment of FBI agents waiting to arrest him there, but there was only Elspeth.

She looked drained. She led him outside to where her white Corvette was parked in the hot sun.

As soon as they were inside the car, he said, 'How's Theo?'

'Pretty shook, but he'll be OK.'

'Do the local police have his description?'

'Yes—Colonel Hide gave it out.'

'Where's he hiding?'

'In my motel room. He'll stay there until dark. What about you? Will the CIA give your description to the police?'

'I don't think so. The Agency likes to solve its own problems. They'll think I've gone rogue, and their only concern will be to take me out of circulation before I embarrass them. Once they start listening to Luke and realising they've been harbouring a double agent, that may make them even more eager to hush things up.'

'So the three of us are still in play. That gives us a good chance to still pull this thing off.'

In twenty-four hours, it would be all over, Anthony thought. They would have struck a historic blow for the cause to which they had devoted their lives.

Elspeth glanced across at him. 'What will you do after tonight?'

'Go to Moscow. I have everything I need—passports, cash, disguises.' Anthony was a major in the KGB. Elspeth had been an agent longer—had in fact recruited Anthony—and she was a colonel. 'They'll give me some kind of senior advisory-consultative role,' he went on. 'After all, I'll know more about the CIA than anyone else in the Soviet bloc.'

'You're not nervous?

'Sure I am. I'll be lonely at first—no friends, no family, and I don't speak Russian. But maybe I'll get married and raise a brood of little comrades.' His flip answers disguised his anxiety. 'I decided, a long time ago, to sacrifice my personal life to something more important.'

'I made the same decision, but I'd still be frightened of moving to Moscow.'

'It's not going to happen to you.'

'No. They want me to stay in place at all costs.'

For the last four years, Russian scientists had known everything about the US space programme thanks to Elspeth. She was the reason the Soviets had beaten the Americans into space. She was easily the most important spy of the Cold War.

Her work had been done at enormous personal sacrifice, Anthony knew. She had married Luke in order to spy on the space programme, but her love for him was genuine and it had broken her heart to betray him.

Among the palm trees on the roadside ahead, Anthony saw a huge model of a space rocket above a sign that read STARLITE MOTEL. Elspeth slowed the car and pulled in, parking as far as possible from the road. The rooms were in a two-storey building around a large pool where some early birds were already sunbathing. Anthony wanted to be seen by as few people as possible, so he pulled his hat low and walked quickly as they went from the car to her room.

Theo was standing at the window. Elspeth introduced the two men. Theo said to Anthony, 'How did Luke find me out—did he explain that to you?'

Anthony nodded. 'He was using the Xerox machine in Hangar R. There's a security logbook beside the machine. You have to note the date and the number of copies you made, and sign the log. Luke noticed that twelve copies had been signed for by "WvB", meaning Wernher von Braun.'

Elspeth said, 'I always used von Braun's name, because no one would question the boss.'

Anthony went on, 'But Luke knew that von Braun was in Washington that day. He went to the mail room and found the copies in an envelope addressed to you. He decided he couldn't trust anyone down here, so he flew to Washington. Fortunately, Elspeth called me and I was able to intercept Luke before he told anyone.'

Elspeth said, 'But now Luke has rediscovered what we made him forget.'

Anthony asked her, 'What do you think the army will do?'

My guess is they'll change the code.'

Anthony said, 'If they change the code we can't make the rocket self-destruct.'

'I have to find out what their plan is, and figure out a way around it.' Elspeth slung her jacket over her shoulders. 'Buy a car. Drive to the beach as soon as it's dark. Park as near as you can to the Cape Canaveral fence. I'll meet you there.' She went out.

After a moment, Theo said, 'You have to give her credit, she's got a cool nerve.'

4.00PM: THE COUNTDOWN stood at X minus 390 minutes. Elspeth moved about the base restlessly, updating her timetable, alert for changes in procedure. So far she had gained no clue as to how the scientists planned to guard against sabotage—and she was starting to feel desperate.

Everyone knew that Theo Packman was a spy and that Colonel Hide had raided the Vanguard Motel with four cops and two FBI men. The space community quickly linked the news with the last-second cancellation of the launch. The explanation given, that a late weather report had indicated a worsening of the jet stream, was not believed by anyone inside Cape Canaveral. As midday cooled into afternoon, Elspeth's tension mounted. If she did not learn the plan soon, it would be too late.

Luke had not showed up yet. She was longing to see him, and dreading it at the same time. She missed him when he was not beside her at night. But when he was there, she thought all the time about how she was working to destroy his dream. Her deceit had poisoned their marriage, she knew. All the same, she yearned to see his face, to hear his grave, courteous voice, to touch his hand and make him smile.

The scientists in the blockhouse were taking a break, eating sandwiches and drinking coffee. She sat next to Willy Fredrickson, her boss, who had his headphones round his neck while he ate a grilled-cheese sandwich. 'I guess you know everyone's talking about an attempt to sabotage the rocket,' she said conversationally.

Willy looked disapproving, which she took as a sign that he knew exactly what she was talking about. Before he could reply, a technician at the back of the room said, 'Willy,' and touched his own headphones.

Willy listened to his headset for a minute. 'OK,' he said into his mouthpiece. Then he looked up and said, 'Stop the countdown. There'll be a ten-minute delay.'

Elspeth lifted her pencil expectantly. 'Shall I say why?'

'We have to replace a feed-through capacitor that's chattering.'

Capacitors were essential to the tracking system, and 'chattering'—small electrical discharges—could be a sign that the device was going to fail. But Elspeth was not convinced.

She scribbled a note, then got up and left. Outside the blockhouse, the afternoon shadows were lengthening. The white shaft of Jupiter-C stood like a signpost to the heavens. She walked briskly across the lawn to the launch pad and entered the steel cabin in its base that housed the offices. The gantry supervisor, Harry Lane, was speaking into a phone. When he hung up, she said, 'Ten minutes delay?'

'Could be more.'

Writing on her pad, she said, 'Reason?'

'Replacing a malfunctioning component,' he said.

Just then, a technician in oily overalls walked in. 'Here's the old one, Harry,' he said. In his dirty hand he held a plug.

Elspeth knew it was the receiver for the coded self-destruct signal.

She walked quickly out of the door before Harry could see the triumphant expression on her face. Heart thumping with excitement, she hurried back to her Jeep.

She sat in the driving seat, working it out. To prevent sabotage they were replacing the plug. The new one would be wired differently, to work on a different code. The new plugs had probably been flown here from Huntsville earlier in the day. The plugs were always made in sets of four, the duplicate pair being a spare in case of malfunction. It was the duplicate pair that Elspeth had examined, last Sunday, when she had sketched the wiring. Now she had to find the new duplicate set and do the same all over again.

She drove fast back to the hangars. She entered Hangar D and went to the telemetry room. This was where she had found the duplicate plugs the last time.

Hank Mueller was leaning on a bench, looking solemnly at a complex electrical device. When he saw her, he brightened and said, 'Eight thousand.'

Elspeth suppressed her impatience. She would have to play the numbers game with him before anything else. 'It's the sum of four consecutive cubes: eleven, twelve, thirteen, fourteen.'

'Very good.' He gave her a dime and looked expectant.

She racked her brains for a number, then said, 'The cube of sixteen thousand, eight hundred and thirty.'

'I can't work that out, I need a computer,' he said indignantly.

'You haven't heard of it? It's the sum of all the consecutive cubes from one thousand, one hundred and thirty-four to two thousand, one hundred and thirty-three,' she said.

'I didn't know that! That's the first time you've ever kept my dime.' He looked comically despondent.

She asked, 'Do you have the duplicate set of new plugs from Huntsville?'

'No,' he replied. 'They put them in a safe.'

She was relieved he didn't question her need to know. 'What safe?'

'They didn't tell me.'

'Never mind.' She went out and hurried to Hangar R. There was only one safe that she knew of—in Colonel Hide's office.

She went to her desk, took an army envelope and typed on it: 'Dr W. Fredrickson—Eyes Only.' Then she slid two blank sheets of paper into the envelope, and sealed it.

She went to Hide's office. He was alone, sitting behind his desk. He looked up and smiled, 'Elspeth,' he said. 'What can I do for you?'

'Would you keep this in the safe for Willy?' She handed him the envelope.

'Sure,' he said. He spun around in his chair and opened a cupboard behind him. Looking over his shoulder, Elspeth saw a steel door with a dial. She moved closer. The dial was graduated from 0 to 99, but only multiples of 10 were marked with a figure, the other numbers being indicated by a notch. The first number where Hide stopped the dial was easy: 10. Then he dialled a number just below 30, either 29 or 28. Finally he moved the dial to between 10 and 15. The combination was something like 10, 29, 13. It must be his birthday, either the 28th or 29th of October, in 1911 to 1914. That gave eight possibilities.

Hide opened the door. Inside were two plugs.

Elspeth smiled as he tossed the envelope into the safe, then closed the door. 'Thank you, Colonel.'

Now she had to wait for him to leave his office. She returned to her own office and her phone rang. It was Anthony. 'We're leaving here in a few minutes,' he said. 'Do you have what we need?'

'Not yet, but I will. What kind of car did you buy?'

'A light green Mercury Monterey, fifty-four model.'

'I'll recognise it.' Colonel Hide passed her door. 'I gotta go,' she said, and hung up.

She went out. Hide stood in the next doorway, talking to the girls in the typing pool. Elspeth loitered, wishing he would move on. But when he did, he returned to his office and stayed there for two hours.

Elspeth almost went crazy. She did not leave her office. Her timetable was forgotten. Willy, her boss, would be furious, but what did that matter? She looked at her wristwatch every few minutes. At eight twenty-five Hide at last walked past. She sprang up and went to her door. She saw him heading down the stairs.

Another man was walking along the corridor towards her. He said, 'Elspeth?' Her heart stopped, and she met his eye. It was Luke.

8.30PM: LUKE HAD BEEN dreading this moment.

He had dropped Billie off at the Starlite. She planned to freshen up then get a cab to the base in time to see the launch. Luke had gone straight to the blockhouse and learned that takeoff was now scheduled for 10.45pm. Willy Fredrickson had explained the precautions the team had taken to prevent the sabotage of the rocket. Luke was not completely reassured. He wished Theo Packman had been arrested, and he would have liked to know where Anthony was. However, neither of them could do anything with the wrong code. And the new plugs were locked in a safe, Willy told him.

Luke would feel less worried when he had seen Elspeth. When he looked into her eyes and asked her to tell him the truth, he would know if his suspicions were correct.

He came up the stairs in Hangar R. As he reached the top he saw a tall redhead emerge from an office along the corridor, looking anxious. She was more beautiful than her wedding photograph.

He spoke to her, and then she noticed him. 'Luke!' She came quickly towards him. Her smile showed genuine pleasure, but he saw fear in her eyes. She threw her arms around him and kissed him.

He cut short the kiss and detached himself from her embrace. She frowned and looked hard at him, trying to read his expression. 'What is it?' she said. Then she sniffed, and sudden anger suffused her face. 'You've been with a woman.' She pushed him away. 'You screwed Billie Josephson, you bastard!'

Her betrayal was worse than his, but anything he said was going to sound like a pathetic excuse. So he said nothing.

Her mood switched again, just as quickly. 'I have to go. We'll talk later.' She looked up and down the corridor, seeming impatient.

'I don't think so,' he said. 'When I was at the house I opened a letter addressed to you.' He took it out of his jacket pocket and gave it to her. 'It's from a doctor in Atlanta.'

She pulled the letter out of the envelope and began to read it. 'Oh, my God,' she whispered.

'You had your tubes tied six weeks before our wedding,' he said.

Tears came to her eyes. 'I didn't want to do it,' she said.

He led her into her office, closing the door. She sat down at her desk, fumbling in her purse for a handkerchief. He pulled a chair over close to her.

'I almost didn't have the operation,' she said. 'It broke my heart.'

He looked carefully at her, trying to be detached. 'I guess they forced you to.' He paused. Her eyes widened. 'The KGB,' he went on, and she stared at him. 'They ordered you to marry me so that you could spy on the space programme, and they made you get sterilised so that you would not have children to divide your loyalties.' He saw a terrible grief in her eyes and knew he was right. 'Don't lie,' he said. 'I won't believe you.'

'All right,' she said.

She had admitted it. He sat back. It was all over.

'I kept changing my mind,' she said, and tears rolled down her face as she spoke. 'In the morning I'd be determined to do it. Then at lunch time I'd call you and you'd say something about a house with a big yard for children to run around in, and I'd make up my mind to defy them, but I couldn't in the end. What are you going to do, now? Call the FBI?'

'Should I?'

'If you do, I'll end up in the electric chair, like the Rosenbergs. But there's an alternative.'

'What?'

'Let me go. I'll go to Europe. From there I can get a flight to Moscow.'

'Is that what you want to do? Live out your days there?'

'Yes.' She gave a wry grin. 'I'm a KGB colonel, you know. I'd never be a colonel in the US.'

'You'd have to go now, immediately,' he said.

'OK.'

'I'll escort you to the gate, and you'll have to give me your pass so you can't get back in.' He looked at her, trying to imprint her face on his memory. 'I guess this is goodbye.'

She picked up her purse. 'Can I go to the ladies' room first?'

'Of course,' he said.

9.30PM: ELSPETH WALKED out of her office, passed the door of the ladies' room, and entered Colonel Hide's office. It was empty.

She closed the door behind her and stood leaning against it, trembling with relief. The office swam in her sight as her eyes filled with tears. The triumph of her life was within her grasp, but she had just ended her marriage to the best man she had ever known, and she was committed to leave the country of her birth and spend the rest of her days in a land she had never seen.

She closed her eyes and made herself breathe slowly. Then she turned the key in the office door, went to the cupboard behind Hide's desk and knelt in front of the safe.

Carefully, she repeated the actions Hide had performed when she watched him opening the safe. She dialled 10, 20, 14. She tried to turn the handle. It would not move. She heard footsteps outside, and a woman's voice, but the footsteps receded and the voice faded.

She knew the first number was 10. She dialled it again. The

second number could have been 29 or 28. She dialled 28 this time, then 14 again. The handle still would not turn.

She had tried only two possibilities out of the eight. Next she tried 10, 29, 13, then 10, 28, 13. She was halfway through the list.

She heard a siren give a warning blast—two shorts and a long. This meant that all personnel should clear the launch-pad area. The launch was an hour away.

The combination 10, 29, 12 did not work. But 10, 28, 12 did. Jubilant, she turned the handle and pulled open the heavy door. The two plugs were still there. There was no time now to dismantle them and sketch the wiring. She would have to take them to the beach. Theo could use the actual plug in his own transmitter.

Someone tried the door and Elspeth stopped breathing.

A man's voice called, 'Hey, Bill, you in there?' It sounded like Harry Lane. What the hell did he want? The doorknob rattled. Then she heard departing footsteps. She grabbed the plugs from the safe and stuffed them into her purse. Then she closed the safe, spun the dial, and shut the cupboard.

She went to the office door, and opened it. She re-entered her office. Luke was sitting where she had left him, looking grim. 'I'm ready,' she said.

He stood up. 'After you leave here, you'll go straight to the motel,' he said. 'In the morning, you'll drive to Miami and get on a plane out of the United States.'

'Yes.'

He nodded, satisfied. Together they went down the steps and out into the warm night. Luke walked her to her car. As she opened the door, he said, 'I'll take your security pass now.'

She handed it over.

'I'll follow you to the gate in the Jeep.' She realised this was goodbye. She found herself unable to speak. She got into her car.

The lights of Luke's Jeep came on and followed her as she drove off. Passing the launch pad, she saw the gantry inching back on its tracks, leaving the huge white rocket standing alone in the floodlights. She checked her watch. It was a minute before ten. She had forty-six minutes left.

She drove out of the base without stopping. The headlights of

Luke's Jeep diminished and finally disappeared as she rounded a bend. 'Goodbye, my love,' she said aloud, and began to cry.

The lights of other cars swept by in blurred streaks. She almost overshot the beach road. When she saw it, she jammed on her brakes and slewed across the highway in the path of the oncoming traffic. A taxicab braked hard and swerved, honking, and narrowly missed the tail of her Corvette. She bumped onto the uneven sand of the beach and drove on, more slowly, to the beach.

AFTER ELSPETH LEFT, Luke stayed at the gate in his Jeep, waiting for Billie. He felt stunned. He had been married to a spy for four years. He could hardly take it in.

Billie arrived at ten fifteen in a taxicab. He signed her in, then they headed for the blockhouse. 'Elspeth has gone,' Luke said.

'I think I saw her,' Billie replied. 'Is she in a white Corvette?'

'Yes, that's her.'

'My cab nearly hit her car. I saw her face in the headlights. She was turning off the road in front of us.'

'She told me she'd go straight back to the Starlite.'

Billie shook her head. 'No, she was heading for the beach.'

'Damn,' said Luke, and he turned the Jeep around.

ELSPETH DROVE SLOWLY along the beach, staring at the groups of people who had gathered for the launch. She was looking for a Mercury Monterey. Anthony had told her it was green, but there was not enough light to see colours.

She started at the end of the beach nearest to the base, but Anthony and Theo were not there. She guessed they had chosen a more isolated spot. She checked her watch. It was ten thirty. She was almost out of time.

Elspeth drove close to a car that looked right, but it seemed to be empty. She accelerated again—then it honked. She slowed down and looked back. A man had got out and was waving at her. It was Anthony. 'Thank God,' she said. She reversed back to him and leaped out of the car. 'I've got the duplicate plugs,' she said.

Theo got out of the other car and opened its trunk. 'Give them to me,' he said. 'Quickly!'

10.45PM: THE COUNTDOWN reaches zero.

In the blockhouse, the launch conductor says: 'Firing command!' A crewman pulls a metal ring and twists it. This is the action that fires the rocket. Prevalves open to let the fuel start flowing. The liquid oxygen vent is closed, and the halo of white smoke around the missile suddenly vanishes.

The launch conductor says, 'Fuel tanks pressurised.'

For the next eleven seconds, nothing happens.

The Jeep tore along the beach at top speed, dodging in and out of family groups. Luke scanned the cars, ignoring the cries of protest as his tyres showered people with sand. Billie was standing beside him, holding the top of the windshield.

The last connection hose drops away from the missile. A second later, the priming fuel ignites, and the first-stage engine thunders into life. A huge orange firelick bursts from the base of the rocket as thrust builds.

With painful slowness, Jupiter-C lifts off the launch pad.

In the blockhouse, someone yells, 'Go, baby!'

Billie saw a white Corvette parked next to a darker sedan. 'There,' she screamed.

'I see them,' Luke shouted back.

At the rear of the sedan, three people were clustered around the open trunk. Billie recognised Elspeth and Anthony. The other man was presumably Theo Packman. Their heads were raised and they were staring across the sand dunes towards Cape Canaveral.

Billie read the situation instantly. The transmitter was in the trunk. They were in the process of setting it to broadcast the detonation signal. She turned towards Cape Canaveral. There was nothing to see, but she heard a deep, rumbling roar like the sound of a blast furnace in a steel mill. The rocket was taking off.

'We're out of time!' she yelled.

'Hold tight!' Luke said.

She gripped the windshield as he swung the Jeep around in a wide arc.

The rocket picks up speed suddenly. At one instant it seems to be hovering hesitantly over the launch pad. At the next it moves like a bullet out of a gun, shooting into the night sky on a tail of fire.

Over the roar of the rocket, Elspeth heard the scream of a car engine. She looked up and saw a Jeep heading for them at top speed. 'Hurry,' she screamed.

Theo connected the last wire. On his transmitter were two switches, one marked ARM and the other DESTROY. Theo threw the ARM switch.

On the beach, a thousand faces tip backwards, watching the rocket rise straight and true, and a huge cheer goes up.

Luke drove straight for the back of the Mercury. The Jeep had slowed as he turned, but he was still travelling at about twenty miles per hour. Billie jumped out, hit the ground running, then fell and rolled.

At the last second Elspeth threw herself out of the way. Then there was a deafening bang and the crash of breaking glass. The Mercury's rear end crumpled and its trunk lid came down with a bang. Luke was thrown forward violently. The bottom of the steering wheel caught his lower chest, and he felt the sharp pain of cracked ribs. His forehead hit the top edge of the wheel, and he sensed blood flowing down his face.

He pulled himself upright and looked at Billie. She seemed to have fared better than he. She was sitting on the ground rubbing her forearms, but she did not appear to be bleeding.

He looked across the hood of the Jeep. Theo lay on the ground, not moving. Anthony was on his hands and knees, looking shaken but unhurt. Elspeth had escaped injury and was scrambling to her feet. She dashed to the Mercury and tried to open the trunk.

Luke leaped out of the Jeep and ran at her. As the trunk lifted, he shoved her aside.

Anthony yelled, 'Hold it!' Luke looked at him. He was standing over Billie with a pistol to the back of her head.

Luke looked up. The red firetail of the missile was a bright shooting star in the night sky. As long as that was visible, Jupiter-C could still be destroyed. The first stage, which contained the explosive detonator, would burn out when the rocket was sixty miles high. It would separate and fall away, eventually to splash down in the Atlantic Ocean. Separation would take place two minutes and twenty-five seconds after ignition. Luke figured the rocket had been ignited roughly two minutes ago. There had to be about twenty-five seconds left, plenty of time to throw a switch.

Luke looked at Billie. She was on one knee, like a sprinter at the starting line, frozen in position with the long silencer of Anthony's gun pressing into her curly black hair. He asked himself if he was ready to sacrifice Billie's life for the rocket. The answer was No.

Elspeth again bent over the trunk of the car.

Then Billie threw herself backwards, hitting Anthony's legs with her shoulders.

Luke lunged at Elspeth and pushed her away from the car.

The silenced gun coughed as Anthony and Billie fell in a heap.

Luke stared in dread. Had Anthony hit Billie? She rolled away from him, apparently unhurt. Then Anthony lifted the gun, aiming at Luke.

Luke looked death in the face, and a peculiar calm possessed him. He had done all he could.

There was a long moment of hesitation. Then Anthony coughed, and blood came out of his mouth. Pulling the trigger as he fell, he had shot himself, Luke realised. Now his limp hand dropped the gun and he slumped back on the sand, his eyes staring up at the sky but seeing nothing.

Elspeth sprang up and bent over the transmitter a third time.

Luke looked up. The firetail was a glow-worm in space. As he watched, it winked out.

Elspeth threw the switch, but she was too late. The first stage had separated. Luke sighed. It was all over. He had saved the rocket.

Billie put her hand on Anthony's chest, then checked his pulse. 'He's dead,' she said.

At the same moment, Luke and Billie looked at Elspeth. 'You lied again,' Luke said to her.

'We weren't wrong,' she yelled hysterically. 'We were not wrong!'

Behind her, families of spectators and tourists were beginning to pack their belongings. No one had been close enough to notice the fighting; all eyes had been turned to the sky.

Elspeth got into her car, slamming the door, and started the engine. Instead of turning towards the road, she headed for the ocean and drove straight into the water.

The Corvette stopped, waves lapping at its fenders, and Elspeth got out. In the car's headlights. Luke and Billie saw her begin to swim out to sea. Luke moved to go after her, but Billie grabbed his arm and held him back.

'She'll kill herself!' he said in agony.

'You can't catch her now,' Billie said. 'You'll kill yourself!'

Luke still wanted to try. But then Elspeth passed out of the headlights' beam, swimming strongly, and he realised he would never find her in the dark. He bowed his head in defeat.

Billie put her arms around him. After a moment, he hugged her back. Standing on the beach, with their arms around one another, they both looked up.

The sky was full of stars.

Epilogue

1968: Luke was on the NASA team that put Apollo 11 on the moon.

By then he was living in a big, comfortable old house in Houston with Billie, who was head of Cognitive Psychology at Baylor. They had three children: Catherine, Louis and Jane. (His stepson, Larry, also lived with them, but that July he was visiting his father, Bern.)

Luke happened to be off duty on the evening of July 20. Consequently, at a few minutes before nine o'clock, Central time, he was watching TV with his family, as was half the world. He sat on the big couch with Billie beside him and Jane, the youngest, on his lap. The other kids were on the carpet with the dog, a yellow Labrador called Sidney.

When Neil Armstrong stepped on the moon, a tear rolled down Luke's cheek.

Billie took his hand and squeezed it.

Catherine, the nine-year-old, looked at him with solemn brown eyes. Then she whispered, 'Mommy, why is Daddy crying?'

'It's a long story, honey,' Billie said. 'I'll tell it to you, one day.'

Explorer 1 was expected to remain in space for two to three years. In fact it orbited the earth for twelve years. On March 31, 1970 it finally re-entered the atmosphere over the Pacific Ocean near Easter Island, and burned up at 5.47am, having circled the earth 58,376 times and travelled a total of 1.66 billion miles.

KEN FOLLETT

Ken Follett was just under thirty years old when his novel, *Eye of the Needle*, hit the best-seller lists in 1978. He has been a name to reckon with ever since, as well as being a great favourite with Condensed Books readers—this is the tenth time one of his books has appeared in the series. *Code to Zero* is Follett doing what he does best: combining heart-stopping fiction with historical fact.

The novel is set in 1958 during the early days of the space programme in the United States. The Soviet Union had already successfully launched the Sputnik satellite in 1957 and the US were attempting to regain their position in the space race with the Jupiter-C rocket. It's a historical fact that Jupiter's launch was delayed twice, and Follett has taken this information, let his imagination run riot, and plotted an exciting thriller around it. Another important element in the novel, the CIA mind-control programme, is also based on fact. Between 1953 and 1963 the US Central Intelligence Agency carried out top-secret research into mind control using drugs, electric shock treatment and sensory deprivation to artificially induce amnesia. It's a chilling but fascinating episode of the Cold War era, and one that Ken Follett has put to good use in *Code to Zero*.

One of the author's great passions in life is politics and he has long been involved with the Labour Party at both local and national level. He has been famously dubbed a 'champagne socialist'—a description he cheerfully accepts. 'I deserve both halves of that label. I've always been enthusiastic about champagne!' His wife Barbara shares his interest in politics and was elected Labour MP for Stevenage in 1997.

Follett's other passion is jazz, and he plays regularly in a blues band. Fans may be interested to know that he can be heard performing vocals and bass guitar on a CD aptly titled *Stranger than Fiction*.

201-001